A KALANU MOUNTAIN MYSTERY

J. THOMAS WITCHER

NATBEN PUBLISHING 2014

ATLANTA, GEORGIA

CHAPTER ONE

Demons filled his mind as he watched the children play.

He thought it would be different this time. He had been promised it would be different. Yet, he could feel the demons growing more powerful with each passing second. He hated the demons. He had struggled against them for as long as he could remember and sometimes he could drive them away with drugs or alcohol, but sometimes he just gave into them. He wanted to give in now, but he struggled to push them into the deepest part of his mind. He knew they would not stay away long. They would return with a vengeance. He only hoped he had time enough.

The spirit of the mountain depended on him.

The children's shouts and laughter made things worse. He reached into the pocket of his thin jacket and tugged out a bottle. There was little whiskey left. Only a few drops trickled onto his tongue and down the back of his throat. It was not enough to keep the demons away. It was not even enough to warm his insides.

He looked toward the mountain. Kalanu Mountain looked dark and forbidding, the peaks covered in a smoky haze. He had heard someone mention the possibility of a January snow and usually the January snows were the worst. And there was a chilled, biting wind that penetrated his clothes and kept him shivering. He felt the cold deep in his bones.

What had his father called it?

Kala Wind.

"The Kala Wind is God's way of reminding us of His power," his father often said. "It is a fearful wind that gets into the marrow of the bones of a sinner, and he'll never be warm again until he reaches the fires of hell."

A sermon that made no sense, but then the honorable Reverend Anton Jessop of the Redeemed Church preached many sermons that made no absolutely no sense to the small, sweating boy on the front row. His father was full of crap about many things, but he was right about the wind. It made you almost long for the fires of hell.

He shivered and tried desperately one last time to get more whiskey out of the bottle but there was nothing. In disgust he hurled the bottle away into the brush nearby. He stood, and stretched and then sat back down.

He was perched on the edge of an old oak stump concealed in a thick grove of pine trees. From his position, he had a clear view of the children playing in the empty lot just beyond the wood. They were playing softball, a dozen kids from the neighborhood, boys and girls, but he was not interested in any of them except the tall, slender blond girl. He kept his eyes on her and when she got out of his sight, he would move position so he could keep his eyes on her. She was a good softball player. She had already hit one ball out into the street beyond the lot, and she had gotten into an argument with a bigger boy who had eventually backed down.

It was easy to see why she was the chosen one.

He only wished they would stop the game. He wished they would all return to the brick and wood ranch-style homes along the street. Shadows were falling. A few streetlights were popping on. Darkness was crowding in around them. Surely their parents would be calling them back inside.

He scratched his skinny, scarred arms. Behind him, something stirred. It might have been the Kala Wind that stirred the high grass or perhaps a small animal venturing out of its burrow looking for food. It could have been anything.

He shivered because he knew there were scary things in the dark.

And he was one of them.

….

"Hope in therapy," Tobias Atkins said out loud.

5

The words were engraved on a metal plate above the door of the large, cream-colored hospital room where he did his morning workouts. He had read somewhere that the cream color was supposed to soothe. He didn't feel soothed. Neither did he feel a lot of hope. Mostly he felt a little lost, sore, and dispirited. He was strapped into a futuristic-looking machine that reminded him of a medieval stretching rack. Modern medicine had taken the place of the Inquisition. At the touch of a button the machine went into convulsive gyrations intended to stretch every muscle to the limit. Or beyond.

At times he felt like a crab about to be cracked for dinner.

He might have felt more comfortable if he could have controlled the button starting the machine, but the button was at the end of a long electrical cord controlled by a very pretty and petite young woman named Agnes. He was positive Agnes was related to the Marquis De Sade. It seemed she enjoyed inflicting pain. It didn't help that her favorite outfit was jeans and T-shirts with slogans like "This won't hurt me a bit" and "pain is good for you."

His chair came back to the starting position and Agnes smiled. She really was very pretty with her green eyes and shoulder-length blond hair and bright smile, but there were times when he saw a devilish glint in her eyes, mostly just before she pushed the button.

"You remind me of someone," Tobias said.

Agnes rolled her eyes. "Oh, haven't I heard that one before. What was her name?"

"He was not a she. His name was Sergeant Roo and he was the senior drill instructor of platoon 154 at Paris Island, South Carolina. He was a six-foot three Hawaiian and his greatest love in life was inflicting pain."

"You can't think I enjoy hurting you," Agnes said seriously.

Her eyes grew wide and innocent, and then she smiled. She thumbed the button and the twisting revolutions started again. This time he wasn't expecting it and he yelped at the sharp, stabbing pain that started at his backside flowing up to his upper spine, and he yelped again as the chair came upright.

6

"This is really good for you," Agnes said sweetly. "And you're doing much better.This machine is so much better than what we used to have."

"Except when you accidentally kill somebody," Tobias pointed out.

Agnes shook her head. "That hardly ever happens and it's really inconvient when it does. You wouldn't believe the paperwork we have to fill out."

"I'll just bet," Tobias said.

He started to say something else but he forgot what it was as she pushed the button once more and his words were cut off as he gasped for air. The stretching of his muscles to the limit of endurance was bad enough, but the chair also pressed back on his chest so that he could barely breathe. Each time he knew he would straighten back up before he suffocated, but each time a rush of panic went through him.

This time when he straightened up, they had company. A woman had slipped quietly through the front doors, as different from Agnes as night and day. She was tall, lithe, with dark hair to her shoulders, and eyes almost as black as night. Like Agnes, she wore snug fitting jeans, but she had on a beaded top with a picture of a snarling wolf and knee-length calfskin boots. There was something intimidating about her, something that made even Agnes step back a little.

"You nearly finished, Swede?" she asked.

"Mr. Atkins has another fifteen minutes in the chair," Agnes said. "After that, he's got water therapy for another hour."

"I've been asked to fetch him," Micki said.

For a moment it looked as if Agnes still might protest, but something in Micki's glance made her hesitate. Instead, she helped to unhook Tobias from the machine and then helped him to his feet. He had to rest a moment. He was always a little unsteady afterwards.

"So this is some sort of rescue operation?" Tobias asked her.

"Sure," she said, shrugging,"just like the Calvary arriving in the nick of time or the Lone Ranger and Tonto."

"Which one are you?"

"Does it look like I'm wearing a mask?

Micki Trueblood was of Italian and Cherokee heritage, and when he looked into her face, he saw the face of his oldest friend. She was the daughter of Matt Trueblood, but nobody had known of her until she showed up unexpectedly on his doorstep a month after Tobias had suffered his injury. Tobias had not known she existed until he opened his eyes. And he was still not completely at ease with her. It was as if she had usurped her father's place, like some sort of minor coup had taken place while he slept in darkness, and now there was a new ruler. He didn't dislike her. He didn't know her really, and he wasn't sure he wanted to.

She had not been accepted by her half-siblings. Matt Trueblood had a son and another daughter. The daughter was a teacher in Blairsville and the son an architect in Atlanta, and from what Tobias knew, they had not been overjoyed to meet her. They had especially not been overjoyed when their father had made her a full partner in his flying business. They could not understand why she would show up after so many years, except for mercenary reasons, but then they did not know what Tobias knew about her.

Tobias had used his connections to research her history almost as soon as he had found out about her. She was rich, the daughter of an Italian actress who had recently passed away. Micki Trueblood had grown up in the fast-paced social whirl of movies, celebrities and money. Her name wasn't as infamous as some other celebrity daughters, but only because her mother had been stricter than some, often tucking her away in convent schools for convenience.

The only real scandal connected with her was a short-lived marriage to a much older man.

He wondered why she had come as he followed her out of the therapy room. The therapy building was part of a small clinic in the community of Mount Rawls, Georgia. In the distance Tobias could see the peak of Mount Rawls, but behind it, he could see an even taller peak. It was the dark, forbidding peak of Kalanu. It was a sacred mountain for both the Cherokee and Creek, a place of legend and myth. Some said even an even more ancient people had lived in the high places. He had spent a lot of his boyhood hiking on the mountain with his grandfather and his best friend. He felt a sudden sense of longing for it, but it was impossible. He could barely walk a hundred yards without gasping for breath.

He had to push himself to catch up with Micki's long, energetic stride.

"Are we in a rush to go somewhere?" He asked.

Micki ignored his question. "Do you need to call Abby?'

"Abby didn't bring me today," he said. "I came in a sheriff's car. She had some work she was behind on. She won't expect to see me until she comes home tonight."

"And she doesn't call to check on you?" Disapproval was in her voice.

""This has been hard on her."

"Sure. But nobody clobbered her with a shovel."

He wanted to say something in his wife's defense, but he couldn't put the words together coherently. It happened often. His thoughts grew jumbled. He would suddenly not remember where he was going or what he was supposed to be doing. It was odd, the things he could remember-like the smell of baking bread in his mother's kitchen or the smell of sawdust and oil in his grandfather's workshop.

But sometimes he could not remember how to tie his own shoelaces.

Micki's car was parked at the curb. It was actually Matt's old car, a battered ugly beast of a hybrid, part Humvee, part truck. It had once been dark blue, but the color had faded, and there were a few rust spots in places. It had oversized tires and a rebuilt engine and it could go anywhere on the mountain as long as there was road enough. It also had a police radio. Matt had done a lot of flying for the Sheriff's department and Micki had taken over the responsibilities. Somewhere on her person she carried a small badge giving her ex-officio status as a lieutenant with the department.

It was one of the things he felt resentment about, that she was given that kind of authority simply because she flew airplanes. Odd, but he had never resented it with Matt.

She opened the door for him and he had to step up to get into the seat. It hurt. He was still feeling the effect of his session in the chair. When he tried to hook the seat belt, his fingers fumbled nervously. She finally moved his hands and buckled it herself. There were times when he felt as ineffective as a baby, and it left him frustrated.

"You haven't told me where we are going." Tobias said irritably.

"Sheriff Abercorn wants you," Micki said.

"Why?"

"A girl named Sharon Bishop was kidnapped from her bed last night. The guy that did it is a kind of clown, a sick one, but a clown. He made a lot of noise breaking into the back room window where Sharon was sleeping. He was seen by several people. He evidently didn't have a real good plan. He got her into his car and there was a high speed chase through Mount Rawls and down Atlanta Highway. He finally ended up going up the old logging road on Kalanu."

"There's no way out of there," Tobias said.

"No," Micki said, "and he had half the county chasing him. Some good old boys got to him first. They slapped him around some and might have killed him if a patrol car hadn't gotten there and saved his sorry life."

"What about the child?"

"There was no sign of her."

"That logging road is a mile and a half of bad road before it reaches the ruins of old Kalanu and dead ends," Tobias said. "He must have thrown her out somewhere along the route. There are a lot of deep ravines and brush along the way."

"That's what Sheriff Abercorn believes," Micki said. "But the guys chasing him swear they didn't have Jessop out of their sight for more than a few seconds most of the way up the hill. Course they had been drinking. He might have had time to stop and throw her out, but they swear he didn't. There was only a little time after he stopped the car at the end of the road, and not enough time to take her far."

"They were drunk?"

"Pretty much."

"Then we can't rely on them as eyewitnesses. Even sober people get the facts wrong. So we have people searching right now?"

"Yes, but only a few deputies. It takes time to get a search started, but people are on the way."

"But why do they want me? I can't help search. It might have escaped your notice, but I'm not much of a hiker anymore."

Micki laughed. "No. They don't want you to help search, but her kidnapper is a creepy little man named Clyde Jessop."

"I never heard of him."

"Yes, you have. The Sheriff says you arrested him once. He's mostly been a small time thief, but he's already been arrested a few times for hanging around playgrounds and fondling little girls. The last time was more serious, and you were the arresting officer."

"I can't remember him," he said.

"He remembers you. He says he'll talk to you and nobody else."

"Why me?"

"I don't know, but that's what he says. In the meantime, those good old boys are talking about hanging him up in a tree and gutting him like a deer. Sheriff Abercorn is playing diplomat."

"Harvey is good at that," Tobias said.

"But I think his heart is on the side of the good old boys," she said.

She drove very fast, maneuvering dangerously through scarce traffic and around dangerously sharp turns. She drove through the main section of Mount Rawls, a community that had grown up around Kalanu College. There was still only one red light and Micki busted through it without using the blue light. It made Tobias a little nervous. Even out of season, there were still a few tourists exploring and Micki came alarmingly close to a few of them.

They passed the stately old Kalanu County courthouse, a massive red brick building. It no longer functioned as a courthouse, but the historic building housed a museum for the historical society. The museum had dozens of exhibits portraying the life and hardships of the first Georgia settlers. Across the street from the courthouse was the Mountain Laurel Café, famous for pancakes. Tobias felt his stomach rumble. He had been looking forward to pancakes after his workout.

A few miles outside Mount Rawls on the Atlanta Highway, Micki turned through the gates of a small, private airport.

The sign at the gate read Trueblood Airport and at the entrance there was a green Vietnam era helicopter mounted on a block of concrete. The insignia on the side was a large purple replica of the Peanuts' dog Snoopy, in combat gear. The helicopter was canted almost over on the side so that one of the long blades brushed the ground. Tobias always got a sense of nostalgia when he passed the helicopter. It was out of another era, his era. The sixties. The Beatles. Rock and Roll and Elvis. Three Dog Night and Woodstock the roar of machine guns. Peace rallies in the street. Hell no, we won't go. War is not good for children and other living things. A confusing, passionate time where there was no middle ground and remembering it made him feel old. Now that Matt Trueblood was gone, it made him feel ancient.

They passed the entrance and Micki drove along a long straight road along a few airplane hangars. The airport accommodated a few private planes and the Trueblood Helicopter Adventures. A jet black Robinson R44 helicopter was parked near the red and white Trueblood building. He thought it looked small and fragile, a delicate version of the war machines he had ridden a lifetime ago.

"These always look like toys to me," Tobias said.

Micki glanced at him with a half-amused smile. "I know it's not a Huey, but it will get us there."

"Sometimes they don't," he said.

CHAPTER TWO

He was not fond of helicopters. He had no sense of panic about them, but only an acute awareness he was riding in a very fragile machine. The feeling of the engine running and the solid swish of rotor blades did not reassure him. The basic helicopter was a tube, a piece of metal stretched over an airframe like Saran Wrap fixed around a wire coat hanger. He knew from experience it crumbled easily and it was not pleasant when the engine stopped or the hydraulics failed and it dropped from the sky like a rock. He was uneasy even with the most competent pilot and he had no idea what kind of skill Micki Trueblood possessed.

He knew she had natural ability, inherited from her father who was the best pilot Tobias ever knew, but he had never been up with her before. She handed him headphones and he watched her closely as she went through her checklist. He put the headphones on but there was little to hear except static. She felt his eyes on her and she looked at him curiously.

"Are you nervous?"

"It's not my favorite form of transportation," he admitted.

"If I were you, I'd be more nervous around garden tools."

"Funny girl," Tobias said.

"And I seem to remember my Dad saying something about you being in helicopters a lot in Vietnam? He said you were some kind of crew chief."

"I was a door gunner," he said.

"And what does a door gunner do?" Micki asked.

A momentary vision went through his head of standing in the open doorway of a helicopter watching the ground pass below and hearing the sudden pinging sound of bullets hitting the metal frame, and then all the other helicopters swarming in like locusts, weapons firing, chopping up land and people for a several hundred yards.

"Just like it sounds," Tobias said. "We stood in a small door looking at the ground and searching for bad guys, and we fired our machine gun when they showed up."

"Sounds exciting."

13

"It wasn't. Do you know what other marines called a door gunner?"

"No," she said.

"Bait," Tobias said.

He heard something like a laugh, and then shuddered inwardly as the helicopter lifted up. He had a sense of free falling and involuntarily reached for his belt to steady himself. It was his imagination. It was a little like being in one of those rides at amusement parks. There was really no chance of falling out.

Well, hardly ever.

Helicopters are designed pretty much to go in every direction and Micki seemed to use them all in the first few moments of taking off. His stomach rebelled. He wished he had some good coffee. He wished he were somewhere else.

"You're white as a sheet, "Micki said. "Relax. Nobody's shooting at us."

"Yet," he said.

"And these things hardly ever crash."

"It's the 'hardly ever' part that bothers me," he said.

With the practiced hands of a concert pianist, Micki eased the small helicopter above the trees and veered off to the south across the college and then the city. Below him he saw people stopping to look up. He saw smoke coming from the chimneys of a few houses. He saw a yellow school bus stopped at the red light. She eased the helicopter more to the south and took it over Helena Falls. He caught a glimpse of a few startled deer running for the brush.

"Harvey has set up a command post at the end of the logging road," Micki said. "He already has a tent set up. He figures he's going to have to spend another night and hot food and a warm place will come in handy for the searchers. The weather people say there's snow coming in."

"The Kala wind," Tobias said.

"What?"

"It's supposedly a corruption of a Cherokee word, but people around the mountain have called it the Kala Wind for years. The bitter wind. The beginning of winter."

"I feel left out sometimes," Micki said.

14

"Why?"

"I can speak five languages. I can tell you where to find the best bread and cheese and wine in shops all over Paris, London and Rome. I know what street you should never walk down alone in Naples at night. But I know nothing of my father's people, and little of their heritage." She glanced at Tobias. "I know you were my father's best friend for all of his life and I know little or nothing about you."

"There's nothing to know about me," Tobias insisted. 'Why don't you tell me about Jessop instead?"

It was his way of avoiding answering the question. An old defensive trick. When faced with a choice, go on the offensive. Explanations and apologies only weakened your position, and he did not want to talk about Matt. Some pain went deeper than a savage blow to the head, some hurts were unspeakable. The woman flying the helicopter was Matt's daughter, but he didn't know her. He had no sense of family with her and talking about Matt Trueblood would be talking about family. It was private.

She was intelligent enough to know what he was doing, but she didn't insist.

"I only know what Sheriff Abercorn told me. He's a creep who liked little girls. You arrested him about ten years ago when he tried to pull a little girl into his car in Mount Rawls. Evidently he's always been something of a clown. He tried to grab the girl in broad daylight and in front of half the community. Some construction workers blocked his car and pulled him out. It was almost like last night. If you hadn't come along, those construction workers might have beaten him to death."

"He got prison time?"

"He had a long record of minor stuff like flashing and hanging around playgrounds, and some theft convictions. This time he got ten years in Reidsville. They actually let him out about three months ago, two years early. He was a model prisoner."

"I'm surprised they didn't beat him to death in prison or stick a knife in him," Tobias said. "Even hardened criminals don't like child molesters very much."

Micki dropped the nose of the helicopter down a few feet and followed Atlanta Highway between the high ridges of Mount

Rawls and then veered to the west as she followed the logging road up Kalanu. Tobias had only quick flashes of the old dirt road among the thick growth of trees. There had never been much logging done on Kalanu, just as there had never been much digging or homesteading.

The helicopter flew low over the area outside Mount Rawls called the Windfall Project. Some people called it the Governor's Folly. The original idea had been a short stretch of scenic highway, somewhat like the stretch between Cherokee, North Carolina, and Gatlinburg, Tennessee. A part of the highway would actually carve off a bit of Kalanu which met opposition from the Federal Park Service as well as a myriad of environmentalists. Study after study had been done, a fortune spent in finding out exactly what impact the project would have on the area, and finally it was decided the impact would be negligible in comparison to the enjoyment a great many people would get from the scenic drive. And of course it would draw more tourists and more money to the area.

At the end of the stretch of highway a combination ranger station, rest area, and museum would be built. There was still a lot of opposition from a great many people and groups, but in October the first shovel of dirt had been turned over. On hand to celebrate was the Governor and dozens of dignitaries. There was a free barbeque afterwards. A local band provided the entertainment.

Then another economic crisis had hit and the opposition had grown more vocal, and the project had come to a halt. Down below, the only thing to mark the place where the road was supposed to begin was a blue tool shed. Some people believe the project would never be completed because the mountain was cursed. A lot of people believed Kalanu was a dark mountain. It was certainly full of myth and mystery, and certainly the abrupt abandonment of the early settlement added to the legend. Old Kalanu was their own version of Roanoke Island, where the settlers just vanished.

In fact, history had forgotten the Kalanu settlement existed until a construction crew had stumbled across the ruins while building the logging road.

And his grandfather had made history even more confusing. His grandfather was a storyteller who had a wonderful ability to create magic with his words. He weaved colorful stories of the mountain and its people, so often powerfully visual, so often frightening and so often untrue.

Below they passed over the few ruins of the old city, stone chimneys sticking like sentinels out of the high grass and weeds. He saw a few parked cars and a police van parked in a wide area at the end of the logging road, and then he saw the large camp tent. Beside the tent was a wide, flat area where a helicopter was already parked. It was a stripped down version of an Apache attack helicopter, small and deadly efficient looking. It was painted green with the local National Guard insignia on the side.

"Uh-oh," Miki said.

"Pilots should never say uh-oh," Tobias said. "Is that uh-oh, we're going to crash?"

"No. It's, uh-oh, jackass at four o'clock."

A tall man in uniform came out of the tent. He wore a starched military uniform. Even from a distance, Colonel Barry Silverman looked like a recruiting poster. In civilian life he was a banker and owner of Silverman Real Estate Agency. He also owned at least half of the new Crescent Mall that was currently being constructed near the county line. He was rich, and politically connected, but what he loved most was dressing up in uniform and playing war games. He had somehow managed to avoid actual combat even though his unit had been called up during the Iraq conflict, but it was obvious he saw himself as Patton charging through Italy, even down to the pearl handled revolver he wore at his side.

"We will need the guard before we're done," Tobias said.

"We need the guard," Micki said. "We don't need him. Dad said he'd last about ten minutes in a real combat outfit. And that doesn't even consider his morals."

"What about his morals?" Tobias asked.

"Never mind," Micki said. "I just wish he wasn't involved."

"Unfortunately, it's a package deal," Tobias said.

Micki put the helicopter down gently next to the Apache and Barry Silverman came to greet them. He went first to Micki's side and acted as if he wanted to help her down. She brushed his hands aside and dropped like a cat to the ground and quickly rounded the helicopter to help Tobias with his belts. Silverman was right behind her.

"You handle that thing like your father," Silverman said. "You should consider joining the guard. We can always use good pilots."

Micki didn't smile or acknowledge the compliment. Tobias thought he understood her dislike for him. Silverman was in his late forties, a handsome man with a wife and three children. He was a successful banker, but what he loved best was playing soldier. He was still a boy playing war games while the real soldiers fought and died in lonely corners of the world. Barry Silverman liked the glory and the glamour but he preferred to do it in a clean uniform. He would not do well in the blood and dirt.

Silverman nodded at Tobias. "Are you sure you are up to this, Swede? We've got a missing girl on the mountain and you don't look all that fit."

"It doesn't look like I've got much of a choice," he said

"Frankly, we're treating the little snake better than he deserves," Silverman said. "What we should do is take him up in the chopper and threaten to toss him out the door if he doesn't tell us where she is."

Tobias sighed. "That only works on the second guy."

Silverman got a puzzled look as Tobias went past him toward the tent. He stumbled on uneven ground and immediately felt a strong hand grasp his elbow. He looked at Micki in surprise. She was very quick. Without her steadying hand, he might have hit the ground.

"What did you mean when you said it only works on the second guy?" Micki asked.

"It's an old Vietnam story."

"Tell me."

"The story goes that some CIA operatives used to take two enemy soldiers up in a helicopter. They'd ask the first soldier a question and if he refused to answer, they'd force him out the door. Then they would ask the second soldier the same question."

"And he would answer," Micki said.

Tobias shrugged. "As I said, it only works on the second guy."

CHAPTER THREE

Sheriff Harvey Abercorn appeared in the doorway of the green canvas tent. He was not in uniform. He wore a black waterproof parka to his knees and a hat that covered his ears. He wore heavy boots encrusted with mud. His hat looked like one of those worn by Chinese soldiers during Korea, but it was a plaid color. Abercorn was smoking a black cigar. A short, round man with a ruddy complexion, he was a chameleon, changing his image with every change of the political wind. He was a Democrat in a county full of Republicans, but he kept getting elected. He left the police work to the professionals and he fought the battles of finance and administration, but Tobias was not fooled. Abercorn had been a police officer for a long time. When Abercorn had started, Kalanu County was a little like the Old West. There were moonshiners in the hills and long-time feuds. Money was scarce and sometimes a single deputy covered vast stretches of area. It was said Abercorn knew where the bodies were buried. It was rumored he had buried a few himself.

Abercorn nodded his head toward Silverman, who had stayed near the helicopters.

"Sorry about him," he said. "I wish we didn't have to deal with him, but I have a terrible feeling we'll need the Guard before this night is through. I don't think the little girl could stand another night on the mountain, especially with the temperature dropping."

"How did he get here so fast?" Micki said.

"Sharon Bishop is the daughter of a captain in the Guard who is currently serving in Afghanistan. Silverman is technically his commanding officer and Sharon's mother called him as soon as she found out her daughter was missing."

"I thought Silverman's entire guard group had returned home," Tobias said.

"The majority of them did, but evidently Captain Bishop is some kind of specialist. He speaks the language or something. He stayed behind when the others came home. It seems Silverman has been checking on Mrs. Bishop to make sure she's all right or something. I guess Silverman has a lot of compassion for the men under his command, and he's going the extra mile."

"Yeah, I just bet he does," Micki said. "He strikes me as a very compassionate sort."

Her tone was sarcastic, and Abercorn gave her a sharp look. It was almost a look of warning. There was some undercurrent of very strong feeling that Tobias didn't understand, but then he had not been a part of things for a long while. He had never had much use for department gossip or for the soap opera plots often generated by people who should have known better.

"Is Jessop inside?" Tobias asked.

"Yeah. He's had coffee and some sandwiches I brought up. He won't tell us what happened to the girl. He said he'll only tell you."

"Why me?" Tobias asked.

"I can only guess. Maybe he thought the two of you bonded or something when you arrested him that last time. It happens. But he's a strange little dude, Swede. There's something missing in him that the rest of us have. I'd call it his conscious, but it's more than that. It's like he's just a shell with nothing inside. Even if he didn't want to talk to you, I might have called you up here anyway. You have a gift with people like that."

"Maybe once I did," Tobias said. "I'm not sure anymore. And I don't remember him."

"You will when you see him," Abercorn assured him.

But he didn't. So much of his memory was gone, or it came slowly back to him in bits and pieces. Clyde Jessop was a small, emaciated man. His face was pockmarked from some bad childhood disease. He had tiny burn scars on his neck and down his arms. He also had prison tattoos, long blue lines etched deeply in his skin.

Jessop had a dark bruise on his cheek and another deeper bruise on his neck where it looked as if someone had gripped him with a stranglehold. He sat in front of a lightweight metal table and held a Styrofoam coffee cup in trembling hands. Jessop also moved gingerly in his chair as if he was in pain. Tobias figured the good old boys had broken a rib or two.

One of those good old boys was stretched out on a blanket in the corner snoring drunkenly. A coat covered him.

In a corner a man in jeans and a thick pullover sweater sat with a shotgun across his lap. He was in his mid-twenties, with shaggy blond hair and intelligent blue eyes. He was casually sprawled in the chair, but Tobias knew he was capable of moving very fast. Owen MacGruder had been the star quarterback at Kalanu High and had played two years at the University of Georgia before he ripped a knee. He had gone into the military, serving in Germany with the military police and he had returned to join the Kalanu County Sheriff's Department. He was currently the acting chief investigator for the department while Tobias was on medical leave.

There were actually several working detectives in Kalanu County but years ago a slot had been added for a chief investigator. He was not called the chief of detectives for some unknown political reasons, and he did not act as a manager. His job was to handle special investigations involving really serious crimes or crimes of a delicate nature where there might be politics involved. Tobias has been exceptional in solving cases, while remaining out of the political infighting.

Abercorn admitted reluctantly that Owen also was pretty good, and he also had the added value of growing up in the area and being a hometown football hero. Abercorn's one complaint was that Owen did not take things seriously enough sometimes.

Owen grinned at Tobias.

"There's a great line from an old Robert Redford movie, 'Jeremiah Johnson,'" Owen said. "It goes that 'some say he's dead and some say he never will be.'"

"What are you blabbering about, Owen?" Tobias said.

"I'm talking about how the legend has returned," he said.

"You're full of it," Tobias said. "I suppose you've eaten all the sandwiches?"

"With the exception of the pineapple ones," Owen said. "I never could find a taste for pineapple sandwiches with mayonnaise. There's something icky about it."

"Icky?"

"I always made my sisters always eat those," Owen said.

Owen had three stunning sisters: Faith, Hope and Charity

People always thought he was kidding when he spoke their names, but Tobias knew the family from way back. He had even gone out with Owens's oldest sister, Faith, but she had the good sense to marry the pastor of Kalanu's First Fellowship Church. He and Faith were still good friends.

Tobias took some of the coffee and wished he hadn't. It was lukewarm and nasty. It had the consistency of motor oil. Still, he forced himself to take another swallow and settled down in the uncomfortable metal folding chair across the table from Jessop. He studied Jessop's face a few moments, trying to get some sort of read on him, some inkling as to why Jessop had asked for him.

When Tobias was a young boy, his mother made quilts as gifts for friends. His mother's quilts were still prized around the mountain and those that remained were considered works of art. His mother had a gift for weaving delicate patterns into the material. His mother called it the soul of the quilt. Sometimes she would make a mistake and the pattern wouldn't be right. Other people couldn't see it, but she could. She would never allow a pattern with a mistake to be given away. Tobias had studied those quilts. He had studied them until his eyes hurt and eventually he would find the error in the pattern. His whole life had become searching for those errors and it had become the guts of his investigative technique. He tried to see the errors in the patterns; the flaws others could not see.

He instinctively knew there was something wrong with the pattern of the kidnapping, something out of focus.

He still did not remember Jessop, but he could make some assumptions. Child molesters were usually molested themselves, and Jessop had all the symptoms. He had nervous hands and eyes, constantly looking around as if expecting someone to attack him. The burn marks on his neck were cigarette burns, either self-inflicted as a form of self-punishment or inflicted by others for their amusement. He would be a sad, pathetic creature to most people, and his dreams would be dark.

He also knew Silverman was wrong. Threatening to throw Jessop out of a helicopter would not frighten the little man. Clyde Jessop was already dead in all the ways that mattered. There was only a dull awareness of life within him. He would react when he was hungry or thirsty or when his ugly needs grew uncontrollable, but his soul was empty. Jessop would not be as frightened of death as some. He might not welcome it, but he would accept it as he had accepted all the other hurts in his life.

"What happened to you?" Jessop said.

Tobias shrugged. "It's a long story and not all that interesting."

"You look like death warmed over."

"Never mind about me. How are you feeling? Those boys knocked you around some. Do you need medical attention?"

"I'm okay," Jessop said.

It was the same answer he would have given if his arms had been cut off. He did not ask for help because it would bring him to the attention of those in power. He liked to stay in the background, in the shadows. It was the way he survived.

"You know we didn't talk very much the last time we met,' Tobias said. "Are you from around here, Clyde? I mean, were you born in Kalanu County?"

"I was born in Gainesville," Jessop said. "My Dad worked in a chicken processing plant. I worked there myself for a while when I was a boy."

"That's really hot, sweaty work."

Jessop nodded, his face showing slight animation for the first time. "I always wanted to be a farmer, you know. I think I could have been a good farmer. I am good with animals, you know."

Tobias's focus was on Jessop. He was aware that Sheriff Abercorn and Micki had settled into seats near the tent entrance, and he was also aware that Silverman had followed them into the tent. Silverman did not sit. The tension in his body was apparent. He stood to one side with his arms folded across his chest. Jessop looked apprehensive.

"So what have you been doing lately, Clyde?" Tobias said, trying to bring Jessop's attention back to him. "Where have you been working since you got out?"

"I was working at the Baptist place," Jessop said. "You know, the park?"

24

Tobias knew where Clyde was talking about. The Southern Baptists had a halfway house and campground near Mount Rawls. It was mostly directed toward alcoholics and drug addicts, but they provided a warm place to sleep, odd jobs around the area, and food.

"Is that where you met Sharon?" Tobias asked.

"No," Jessop said, shaking his head vehemently.

"Come on, Clyde," Tobias said softly. "Where did you see her? Did you follow her home from school? Was she walking down the street? Where did you meet her?"

"I never met her," he said. "I never saw her before today."

"That's hard to believe, Clyde."

"I never saw her. I never met her. Kalanu told me where she lived."

"What the hell do you mean?" Silverman finally exploded.

He was unable to control himself any longer. He took two strides across the room and leaned across the table and grasped Jessop by the front of his T-shirt. For a moment Tobias thought he was going to slap Jessop in an act reminiscent of Patton slapping the soldier in the infamous incident in World War Two. Tobias felt suddenly very tired. He had witnessed this before, back before his injury. Silverman was a showman, constantly trying to be the center of attention. Tobias suspected deep down he was insecure. Deep inside was a child who was always afraid he was going to be picked last when they chose up sides for the softball game.

"Barry," Abercorn said softly.

"We brought Swede up here like this little turd wanted, but we don't have all day to play around. There's a little girl out there, hurt, maybe dying, and cold. We've got to find her."

"We're all very aware of that, Barry," Abercorn said. "Now why don't you relax and let Swede do his job? This is what he's good at."

"I hear he's not good at anything anymore," Silverman muttered.

Tobias heard a little gasp from Micki, but he was not really listening to Silverman's words. His focus was still on Jessop. The damage had been done. Jessop had crossed his arms across his chest. His face was empty of expression. He had retreated back inside his own mind, into that cold, dark place that gave him protection from the predators of the world. Jessop may have been a predator himself, but he had spent a lifetime avoiding bigger and more dangerous predators.

"You need to take a deep breath and calm down, Barry," Abercorn said.

"I say we beat the truth out of him," Silverman said.

"Why don't you and I take a walk, Barry," Micki suggested.

Tobias looked at her in abrupt surprise. There was a change in her. For one thing, she was smiling. Tobias had known her only a few weeks before his injury and an only a short time after he had opened his eyes, but he knew she smiled seldom. Her smile made her look softer, more feminine. She looked less grim. When she stood, there was even a subtle change in her posture, in the arch of her hips, in the way she thrust her chest out against the beaded shirt. All three men were suddenly, vividly, aware of her as a woman. It was a transformation only an experienced stage actor could have made in just a few seconds. She made Silverman forget his anger entirely and he responded like a teenage boy flirting with a girlfriend.

"You don't want to stay in here and listen to this," Micki said. "Let's get some fresh air."

Micki leaned forward and whispered something to him that made him laugh. He allowed her to tug him out of the tent.

"That was sort of nauseating," Harvey Abercorn said.

"He did not open his mouth, but was led like a lamb to the slaughter," Tobias said.

"I'm not sure what's what the Prophet meant when he wrote those words, but it fits."

Tobias turned his attention back to Jessop.

"All right, Clyde. The man was right about one thing. We have wasted a lot of time. Why did you want to see me?"

"Because none of the rest would understand."

"Why would I?"

"Because you know the old stories. Your grandfather told you. You know the truth."

"They were just stories, Clyde."

"No. You know it was more than that. You'll understand that I wasn't going to hurt that child."

"How can I understand that? "

"Because I took her to him," Clyde said.

"To him?" Tobias asked, puzzled. "You mean you brought her to somebody on the mountain? There was nobody else there, Clyde."

"He was there. He was there waiting for her. He swooped down out of the sky and he grabbed her and he took her across the three rivers to the Cloud Place."

"He's talking nonsense," Abercorn said.

"Who was it that took her, Clyde," Tobias insisted. "Who?'

"The Raven took her," Clyde Jessop said. "He took her: Kalanu Ahkyeliski."

"I don't understand any of this," Abercorn said. "What is he talking about?"

"He's saying a witch took her," Tobias said.

CHAPTER FOUR

The tent provided little warmth and Jessop was shivering in his thin shirt. Tobias asked Owen to fetch some blankets from one of the patrol cars. Owen returned and draped the blankets around Jessop's frail shoulders. Tobias tried the coffee again and made a grimace of distaste. Deep down he was afraid Silverman was right. Jessop was lying and he had dropped the broken body of Sharon in a ravine somewhere. But something troubled him. He had a developed instinct for detecting truth and lies and there was something in Jessop's voice that said the twisted little man believed what he was saying.

"Let's start at the beginning," Tobias said. "You broke into Sharon's bedroom, and you kidnapped her. You don't deny that?"

"No," Clyde Jessop said. "But it was because Kalanu told me to."

"How?" Tobias said.

Jessop shook his head as if he didn't understand the question.

"How did Kalanu tell you? Did he write it down? Did he take an advertisement out in the prison newspaper? Did he announce it on television? Did he speak in a voice in your ear? How did Kalanu tell you?"

"You don't believe me," Jessop said.

Tobias knew he had made a mistake and let his feelings show in his voice.

"I'm trying to believe you," Tobias said. "The problem is there's so much evidence against you. You said Kalanu told you to take her. But nobody saw anybody else. You were alone when you broke into Sharon's bedroom and alone when they found you up here. Maybe you didn't intend to hurt her. Maybe things just happened."

"I told you I didn't hurt her," Jessop insisted.

"Okay, then tell me how Kalanu spoke to you?"

"He just told me, that's all. He told me Sharon was the chosen one."

Tobias didn't like the choice of words. The chosen one sounded like a mandate from God. It sounded like voices in the head. People who heard voices made him nervous. He had spent too much of his life dealing with people who heard voices advising them to rape and murder.

"You should understand," Tobias said. "Your grandfather knew Kalanu."

"My grandfather was a storyteller," Tobias said. "Sometimes he made up his stories."

"He knew Kalanu," Jessop insisted.

"You said the Raven took her to a Cloud Place?" Tobias asked. "I've never heard of a Cloud Place. I don't remember my grandfather talking about such a place even in his stories. Where is this place?"

"I don't know. It's where Kalanu lives. I don't know where it is."

Tobias sighed. "Okay. Let's start again. From the beginning. I want to know everything you did until the moment the Raven took Sharon."

Tobias spent the next forty minutes going over every detail of Jessop's day from the time he awakened to when he reached the top of the old logging road. There was so much in Jessop's mind that was mixed up with myth and fable. Tobias doubted even Jessop could remember the real truth anymore. Finally, Tobias gave up. The questioning had left him pale and shaken. His head was beginning to hurt. His lukewarm coffee was ice cold. Mathis herded Jessop out of the tent and into the back of the patrol car. He would drive him down to the county jail.

Abercorn put his hand on Tobias's shoulder. "I'm sorry, Swede. I thought bringing you up here was a good idea. I thought it would save time. I guess I'm still thinking it's the old days and you could walk around a crime scene and see something nobody else could see. I should have just taken him down the mountain and let you talk to him in jail. It would have accomplished the same thing and the county wouldn't have had to pay for a helicopter ride."

"Where is his car parked?" Tobias said.

29

"His car? Why?We've gone over that car. There's nothing in it."

"Show me his car," He insisted.

It was not really the car Tobias wanted to see, although he took a look at it when they reached it. It was an old Ford, rusted mostly, with bare tires and one busted taillight. Inside was cluttered with candy wrappers, fast food wrappings and empty beer cans. The dashboard was empty and so was the trunk, not even a spare tire.

"Who does it belong to?" Tobias asked.

"The VIN number shows it was wrecked a long time back. The last title belonged to a garage that went out of business ten years ago. It was probably abandoned somewhere. There are a few of those around."

The front edge of the Ford was wedged against a tree, the fender crumpled. It looked as if it had struck the tree very hard. All the doors were wide open.

"Were the doors open when the good old boys got here?"

"They said they were."

"Where was Jessop?"

"They said he was just standing by the car looking off into the darkness. No sign of the child."

Tobias shook his head as if to clear away the cobwebs, but the cobwebs were still there. Along with a growing headache. He let Harvey walk him back to the warmth of the tent. He settled into the hard, uncomfortable chair.

"What are you thinking?" Harvey asked.

"He wasn't alone in this," Tobias said.

"What?"

"He had a partner. There are a lot of things I can't remember, Harvey. Sometimes it's frustrating and it's like learning to think all over again. But I am sure of this. Clyde Jessop is no historian, and probably not much of a book reader. He knew things about this mountain, knew things about my grandfather, he should not have known. Someone told him. Someone helped him."

"Someone who Jessop thinks is a witch?"

"I believe so," Tobias said.

Harvey shook his head. "Come on, Swede. There was absolutely no sign of anyone else and remember there was very little time for Jessop to hand the girl off to someone else, unless, of course you believe that some witch swooped down and took her off to the cloud place. He's either desperate or delusional."

'Probably both," Tobias said. "But I still think there was someone else."

"But who and how?"

"I don't know. My head is full of fog. For example, Jessop mentioned the witch taking Sharon to a Cloud Place. I don't remember any place called a Cloud Place on Kalanu Mountain."

"And with all your knowledge, if you don't remember it, it's not there."

Tobias shook his head. "There's so much I don't remember. But there may be someone who can. Someone who can separate fact from fiction, reality from myth. She knows these mountains better than anyone alive. She might even have known them better than my grandfather.'

"You're talking about that lady that teaches out at the college. The one they call Mad Hattie."

"Hattie MacDonald, yes."

"I could have Micki take you by the college, but are you sure it's a good idea. You're looking kind of pale. The best thing would be to give somebody else your questions and let them ask. Owen could handle it."

"That's not the way it works," Tobias said.

"Oh yeah, you've explained that before. It's that patterns thing. Are you sure that's what it is or maybe you're just trying to feel like a policeman again."

"I have to talk to her myself. I don't know the questions I want to ask until I hear some of her answers. You know it's the way I work."

"Okay," Abercorn said, "but I'm telling Micki to watch you close. You get any paler and she's taking you home. I don't need you passing out on my watch. I'd never hear the end of it from Abby.'

Micki came back into the tent and they heard the big National Guard helicopter warming up and then lifting off. Tobias

31

realized he had not seen a pilot so Silverman must have been operating the chopper himself. He was surprised Silverman had the skills required.

"He's not a good pilot," Micki said, as if reading his mind. "He flies it with wooden hands and he doesn't think ahead. If anything ever goes wrong up there, he'll be in serious trouble."

"He's leaving sort of abruptly," Abercorn pointed out.

"He suddenly remembered he had an important appointment, but he would be bringing his people back up very soon."

"And you didn't do anything to scare him away?" Tobias asked.

Micki spread her arms out wide. "What could I have possibly done?"

Tobias would have preferred riding back down the mountain in a patrol car or in the battered SUV he saw parked nearby, but the helicopter was faster and he had a dull, dead feeling that time was quickly running out for Sharon Bishop. Even in the short time he had been inside the tent, it had grown colder. His thin jacket was no longer enough.

"You're staying up here?" Tobias asked Abercorn.

"I've got to get the search mobilized for real," Abercorn said. Jack Mathis is coming up with more food, radios, equipment, and supplies. I need to round up the three drunken fools who are still stumbling around the mountain somewhere and pack them in their SUV and get them started home. I figure they'll be ready to go now. I'm also having Mathis bring a better map and I'm going to start marking off some grid searches. You figure Silverman's right and we confine the search to the logging road for now?"

"Until we know anything different." Tobias said. "Right now that makes as much sense as anything."

"I thought we'd get more information from Jessop," Abercorn said. "I hate to admit it, but I figure Silverman's right about him too. He's using us to gain more time. And he's taken so many drugs and drank so much through the years that his brain is fried. Hell, maybe he does believe what he's saying."

"I believe he does," Tobias said.

"But it doesn't make them true because he believes it," Abercorn said.

"No," Tobias admitted.

The helicopter ride back down the mountain was much like the trip up except Micki stayed closer to the trees. At the bottom of the logging road they saw half dozen green military trucks lined up. Silverman may have been a lot of bad things, but he was an excellent administrator. He had mobilized his group very quickly and the first soldiers were starting to arrive. Soon the mountain would be thick with soldiers, deputies, and volunteer civilians, but unless they found the child soon, darkness would close in again and Sharon would spend another long, cold night on the mountain, if she were still alive.

Unfortunately, the more likely scenario was that she was already dead and flung like so much refuse by the side of the logging road. Tobias closed his eyes as Micki brought the helicopter in for a landing at Trueblood Airport. His headache was worse and he was aware of a dull weariness inside. He had spent a lifetime hunting down men like Clyde Jessop. He had seen too much of the dark side of people. He thought about what Abercorn had said about wanting him back, and he wondered if he wanted to go back.

Feeling the engine vibrations ease, Tobias opened his eyes again. The airport was no longer deserted. Silverman's National Guard Huey was parked in the distance, along with a colorful red helicopter of a type Tobias didn't know. He did recognize the wide circle insignia on the side with the initials of a television station in Gainesville.

"The voice of the mountain has a new helicopter," Tobias said.

"I'm impressed," Micki said, but she didn't sound impressed.

Evidently word was starting to get out and there were half a dozen cars parked along the street and a few television vans, one from Atlanta. Reporters were everywhere. One of them was a tall, attractive brunette who came rushing toward them. She tottered dangerously on very high green stiletto heels.

Her luxurious black hair fell to her shoulders. Her makeup was professionally done. Her smile was perfect and very expensive. Her eyes were a dark brown. Her lips seemed set in a perpetual pout. Her expensive looking outfit was two-piece, a beige color, form fitting, and the skirt was mid-thigh. The jacket was open and her white blouse was daringly low cut to show off a great deal of cleavage. Her face was familiar, especially to people in the North Georgia mountains. Tracie Clavier was the nightly news anchor for a local Gainesville television station, TVOM, the voice of the mountain. She also did several radio commercials for local products, and her deep, sultry voice was unmistakable.

"Swede," she said. "Oh, darling, I didn't know you were up and about. It's so good to see you. Are you in this? Tell me about the missing girl."

As Tracie came closer, Tobias saw a flicker in her expression, a breakdown of her usual unshakable composure. Tracie's carefully made up face and fixed smile were her tools of trade, and she had seen enough of life's disasters so that very little shook her complacency. But she hadn't seen Tobias since his injury. She had pretended to be his friend for a long time, but as soon as he was in a coma, he was old news. He could tell she was shaken by his appearance. He remembered her telling him one time, over lunch, that she found him a very good-looking, an almost irresistible man. It was a good thing they were both married. She had spoken the words with her best seductive pout, with an implication, that even married, she might be willing to change her mind under the right circumstances.

He could see she didn't feel that way anymore. He knew what he looked like. He still didn't like looking at himself in the mirror. The scar on the right side of his face was not that bad. It had healed and gave a more severe appearance, like a dueling scar. His blond hair had come back with a few streaks of white, but even that was sort of attractive, or so Abby had said. It was mostly the weight loss that gave him his macabre appearance. He looked skeletal.

"I had been planning to come see you, Swede," Tracie said. "I heard you were out of the coma."

"Nearly four months," Micki pointed out.

34

Tracie turned her head to acknowledge Micki. It was a brief gesture. Tracie's seductive appeal seldom worked as well with women.

"Have you been looking for the missing child?" Tracie asked.

Tracie's cameraman was behind her, pointing his camera.

"Investigator Atkins has been giving us some valuable information concerning the area," Micki said quickly, "but he's still officially on sick leave and he's exhausted. I'm taking him home."

Some other reporters were realizing something was going on and were hurrying across the airport toward them. Tobias had a moment of panic as he felt his thoughts becoming confused. People were crowding in closer. He stopped a faltering step backwards and once again felt Mick's strong grip on his elbow.

"What about the little girl who's missing?" Tracie asked. "What can you tell us about her?"

"We're not at liberty to comment on anything yet," Micki said. "Sheriff Abercorn will be holding a press conference soon."

It was not enough. The reporters wanted more. They followed close as Micki kept her grip on Tobias's elbow and moved him toward her car. At the car Micki opened the door and they once again found themselves surrounded by reporters pressing tightly. Tracie was trying to get her microphone into Tobias's face. He drew back. Micki stepped between them.

"I'm not officially a Kalanu County deputy," Micki said. "They give me a badge and a gun and let me drive the helicopter in searches and rescue operations, but I don't generally make arrests or chase bad guys and I don't have to be politically correct. All of you need to move out of my way or I'm going to get very upset."

It was the longest speech he had heard Micki give and Tracie Clavier stood there only a moment more and then she gave way. So did the rest. Micki's voice was soft but there was something threatening in it, something explosive. Tobias had the same sense that everyone else did. He didn't know what she was going to do if people didn't move, but it was going to be bad. Nobody wanted to make Micki Trueblood angry.

Micki started the car and eased through the crowd. At the entrance she turned right.

"The college is the other way," Tobias pointed out.

"I'm going to feed you first," Micki said. "You look like you're about to pass out. How does the Black Kettle sound?"

"Like a ham and cheese omelet and good coffee," Tobias said.

"I wonder if Silverman gave them an interview when he landed?" Micki said bitterly.

"More than likely," Tobias said.

"Yeah, he wouldn't be able to resist Tracie's charms and a lot of them were showing. I really don't like that woman."

"You've only lived in this county for a year and some months," Tobias said. "How do you know her?"

Miki looked over at him. "That's right. You were in the coma. You don't know."

"What don't I know?"

"She did a really ugly story about Dad when you were in the coma. She made me look like an abandoned daughter. She didn't mention that Dad knew nothing about me. It was a real hatchet job, and I think it hurt Dad a lot."

"And I always thought she was kind of attractive."

Micki looked at him suspiciously.

"Oh, Swede," she said. "Not you and her?"

"If we did, I don't remember," he said quickly.

"Oh, I think you'd remember," Micki said. "It would be like having a leg amputated or hearing you have cancer. Some things are so bad, you'd never forget."

CHAPTER FIVE

She was not cold. Ever since she had awakened to see the terrible man standing over her and had felt the stinging in her arm, she had not felt cold. She had been drowsy, half asleep, for most of the trip and now she was lying on a small cot underneath a pile of blankets. She had no idea where she was. It was a shelter fashioned of long pieces of tree limbs interlaced with thick vines. It was open to the wind, but it was covered enough to keep most of the rain off her. She could see fluffy white clouds. They had been studying clouds in school. She closed her eyes and tried to remember the names of the clouds, but all she could think about was her stomach. She was hungry.

Earlier, she had tried getting up but she was still in her night clothes and pulling the blankets back meant exposing herself to the biting cold. In moments she was shivering uncontrollably and she quickly snuggled back into the cocoon the blankets made.

She had also discovered something else. Wrapped around her ankle was a tight leather band. The band was attached to a very short piece of chain that was attached to a metal rod driven into the dirt floor. She had pulled on it, but there was no give. It would take a greater strength than hers to pull up the rod.

Outside, she heard something or someone moving around.

"Hello," she said. "Hello, someone, please."

There was no answer.

She hadn't seen anyone since she had awakened. She did not remember very much about the night. There were moments when she had drifted in and out of consciousness. She remembered police sirens. She remembered the man cursing. But it was all she remembered. She was smart enough to know she had been given some kind of drug to make her sleep, and her ears were popping like they had been when she had gone on the plane to see her daddy get his medal in Washington, so she thought she was probably high up.

She was on a mountain, but she didn't know which one.

She knew there was Mount Rawls, where she lived and there was Blood Mountain at the state park where her daddy took

them camping sometime and on a school trip she had visited
Brasstown Bald, which was the highest mountain in Georgia.

And, there was Kalanu Mountain.

She shivered. She did not want to be on Kalanu Mountain.
She had heard the stories of how witches lived on Kalanu
Mountain and they disguised themselves like birds and they ate the
hearts of little children. She did not want her heart eaten. She
suddenly remembered she had two library books that were due and
she was going to be late bringing them back.

Mrs. Stephens got very upset at late library books.

And she was supposed to get on the computer with her
daddy this weekend. Her daddy would be upset. She missed him
terribly and loved every opportunity to talk to him. Through the
marvel of technology, she could see his face and hear his voice on
the computer screen.

She wanted to go home.

She heard a noise again outside.

"Hello," she said. "Is anyone there? Please help me."

Again, there was only silence.

And she thought of something else.

How was she going to go to the bathroom?

.....

The Black Kettle Restaurant was located at the turnoff from
Atlanta Highway onto the scenic William B. George Highway. The
highway was named for a former state senator who had worked
very hard to increase funding for education and teacher's salaries
in the Appalachian Region of North Georgia. The highway passed
over Mount Rawls in some of the most beautiful glimpses of
nature in the area, even passing close to a natural waterfall at one
section of road. The Black Kettle was the last place to eat or get
gas before the twenty mile route, and it did a good business. A
dozen cars and trucks were parked in the front when Micki turned
into the parking area.

The restaurant was a rustic timber and stone building with a
feeling of antiquity about it. It fit with the natural look of the land,
as if it had grown up just as the wide trees and shrubbery around it.
It was a good design and made people feel as if they were walking
into a historic building, but in truth was only five years old. Walt

38

Pappas had retired from the restaurant business and moved to the mountains for peace and quiet, but found he couldn't stop working. He had the Black Kettle built to his specifications and hired local people as cooks and waitresses and served good, hot, country food in generous portions. The restaurant was open from early to late seven days a week and it seemed Walt Pappas was always there.

He was a short, stocky man in his mid-seventies, but he had the agility and energy of a much younger man. He greeted them at the door with a bear hug for Micki and then shaking Tobias's hand enthusiastically. Tobias was surprised at the hug. Micki seldom hugged or even shook hands, but there was something overwhelming about Pappas's personality. He was immediately likeable, almost like a best friend you had known all your life.

"Have you found the little girl?" Pappas asked. "I was listening on the radio."

"Not yet," Tobias said.

"Bad thing," Pappas said. "It's a really bad thing. Not even safe in your own beds anymore." Pappas grabbed menus from a hanging file near the front door and walked them through the restaurant to a table in the back near the window. They were near the fire and it was pleasantly warm. Tobias even liked the sound of the fire.

"It's getting colder outside," Pappas said. "Weatherman says there will be snow tonight or tomorrow. Everyone is hurrying to the grocery stores for bread and milk. I'm probably going to close early. They will be closing off the scenic highway soon."

Pappas gave Tobias a sad look. "I'll send the waitress over. You need meat on your bones. You still don't look healthy."

"I'm working on it," Tobias said.

"You eat a lot," he said. "Keep eating. You need your strength if you're going to search for that little girl."

"Not much chance of that happening," Tobias said. "There will be plenty of young men and women searching up there. "

Pappas shook his head. "I know you. You're like me. You can't stay away from the work. You will go where you're needed. It's a shame Matt's not here. He knew the mountain better than anyone, even more than you."

"I know," Tobias said.

"He would know where to look," Pappas said.

Pappas went off to fetch the waitress. Tobias met Micki's eyes and looked away. Matt might know. Matt might remember where the Cloud Place was if he were alive. More and more he felt a growing sense of frustration about things he could not remember.

In a moment a pretty young girl had brought them coffee and taken their order. Tobias ordered an omelet and a glass of orange juice. Toast and grits. He wasn't sure he could get through it all, but he would try. He had a good appetite, but it seemed he could only eat a few bites at a time.

"You think he would know," Micki said. "My dad."

"Probably."

"You don't like talking about him," Micki said. "Or is it that you don't like talking about him with me?'

The waitress brought their food and Tobias was glad of the opportunity not to talk about Matt. He was also right about the food. He felt so hungry, but he could only manage half the omelet and a few bites of toast before he felt stuffed. He drank lots of the coffee. It was ten times better than what he had tasted on the mountain and it was hot.

Micki finished off the last few drops of her coffee and shook her head when the waitress stopped by to offer her another refill. "It was kind of a shock to come here and find that my father had lived a long life, married, had children, and I was not a part of it. It was a very strange sensation to meet my siblings."

"I'm sure it was a bit uncomfortable for you,' Tobias said.

"Tell me about him," Micki said. "You were his best friend. You know more about him than his children."

"I really can't have this conversation," Tobias said.

He knew she wished to talk about her father. It was natural, and Tobias knew she would still be uncomfortable talking about him with her siblings, even if they would talk to her. He knew she would still felt like an intruder, and he wished he could help. But how could he explain to her that he was filled with an unfair sense of betrayal that Matt had died while he was in the coma. His best friend had died while he was deep in darkness, and he had not been able to say goodbye. Perhaps if there had been a gravestone or a cemetery to visit, he might be able to grieve properly, but Matt's ashes had been scattered on the top of Kalanu Mountain.

Micki studied his face thoughtfully for a moment, and then she nodded. "Okay. But we will have this conversation sooner or later. I want to know who my father was."

"Sometimes I'm not even sure who *I* am," Tobias said.

CHAPTER SIX

"How did you end up a pilot, Micki?" Tobias asked. "It seems to big a coincidence."

Micki glanced at him. "So it's okay to talk about *me*?"

"Everybody in Kalanu County is curious about you. "

They were on their way over to the college and their interview with the woman everyone called Mad Hattie. For someone who had not lived in Kalanu County for long, Micki seemed to know all the back roads and shortcuts.

"What's there to know?" Micki said. "I was a mistake of my father and an inconvenience to my mother. I suppose I could say I was lucky that my mother was Catholic or I might not be here at all. In a way, I was lucky twice. I was born in the United States and possess dual citizenship only because my mother was involved in a movie in California at the time of my birth."

"But your love of flying," he said, "surely that's too much of a coincidence."

"I didn't know who he was, but I knew my father was a pilot. As my mother used to put it, 'your father was a magnificent man in uniform and he drove those wonderful flying machines.'"

Micki's voice had taken on a slight singsong Italian accent, a perfect mimic of some of the women Tobias had heard in the black and white movies where some poor actress was trying to sound Italian. Because her Italian heritage was less apparent than her Native American ancestry, it was odd hearing the words come out of her mouth.

"Your mother really talked like that?" Tobias asked.

"But of course," Micki said. "She was an actor. Everything for her was bigger than life, and everything was also a crisis. For her, there were truly no small parts. She gave her all to everything she did."

"And you loved her?"

42

"As every child loves a parent, but she was not a person who welcomed a lot of emotional entanglement. When I was a little girl, I loved being around her on the set. I loved watching her work. For most of the year I lived in a Catholic convent, but all my holidays were spent with my mother in exotic locations around the world. Those were good times."

"And your mother named you Micki?"

"If you must know, Michaela Magliano was the name on my birth certificate, the story goes that my mother had some actor friends visiting one afternoon and she decided to introduce me to them. In the back yard, they found me up in a tree, in nothing but my underwear. I was only seven at the time. One of the actors was Sean Connery and he said I was more a Micki than a Michaela and I was Micki from then on."

"I can't believe it. You were named by James Bond?"

"It's true. And I never felt comfortable with Michaela. I like Micki better. My mother never called me that, but everyone else did. Mother once said she wished her dear Sean had never called me that. It sounded vulgar, like a street urchin."

"But I think you do have your mother's gift. You are a bit of a chameleon. I saw it back in the tent when you suddenly pretended to be Silverman's best friend. That took acting ability. Perhaps you could have been a great stage actor like your mother."

"No. It wasn't for me. I like flying airplanes. I think I would have been in the military if I could have handled the discipline. But I like the planes."

"You never tried acting?" Tobias asked.

"For a time. I loved flying more than acting. I was in a few plays with my husband."

"The older man," Tobias said.

Micki arched an eyebrow. "You've been checking up on me. Does it shock you to know I married a man much older?"

"Nothing much ever shocks me anymore," Tobias said.

"Yes, but I saw the slight raising of the eyebrows. Perhaps not shock, but disapproval."

"Only a half century ago, girls in these mountains married at thirteen and mostly to much older men because the older men were good providers."

"Well, my husband was not a good provider. He was also a bad husband. I was a foolish girl. My mother warned me. I thought he was charming but I soon discovered his favorite past time was complaining about how badly the world had treated him and then he would get drunk and beat me up. Finally, one day I decided he wasn't going to hit me anymore."

"And?" Tobias asked.

"He stopped hitting me," Micki said.

There was something final in her words and Tobias didn't ask anymore. Micki made the turn off the road onto the campus of Kalanu College. Tobias had always believed Kalanu College was the prettiest campus he had ever seen. It was technically Kalanu University now since it could confer graduate degrees, but it had only been a junior college when Tobias had attended. He had finished up his last two years at Georgia State in Atlanta, but he wished he could have stayed and finished at Kalanu. The school had not really grown a lot. It had suffered as all colleges had during the long economic struggles, and it had not completely recovered. But the administrators of the college were smart financially, and they had kept debt low and the school's admission prices economical. They had also built some very attractive red brick dorm buildings on campus and they were kept nice by strict rules that covered just about every indiscretion a college- aged person could think of; rules enforced by no-nonsense house parents, who were usually retired military, and scary. The educational qualifications were high and there were no organized sports teams. It was a school where parents felt good sending their kids and where most of the students enjoyed four years of school on a quiet, pretty campus with a gorgeous mountain backdrop.

Of course, there were those who said it wasn't a true college experience without the pep rallies and drinking parties, the fraternities and sororities, the social fabric and networking of some bigger schools, but it offered a good education at economical prices and it seemed a very good tradeoff to Tobias.

Mad Hattie McDonald was outside the door waiting for them. A slim, attractive woman in her mid-fifties, her hair was bright red touched with silver and she had the pale, fair skin of the natural redhead, easily sunburned. She wore a lightweight pants

44

suit of the same green color of her eyes. Tobias liked her quick smile.

Tobias had never met her personally, but he had listened to her lecture a few times. Her knowledge about Kalanu County and the history of Mount Rawls and Kalanu Mountain, and even of the beginnings of the Appalachian Trail was impressive. It equaled or even surpassed his grandfather's knowledge, but of course she kept her history accurate. His grandfather had been known to twist history to suit his story.

"You look like your grandfather a little," Mad Hattie said, shaking his hand. She glanced at Micki, but it was not in the intimidated fashion a lot of people showed when they met her the first time. Mad Hattie's glance was more speculative.

"Is that a dueling scar?" she asked.

Micki touched her cheek involuntarily, and then laughed. It was a very small scar under her eye, just a small white streak that Tobias thought made her face look more interesting. He had not thought of it as a dueling scar.

"It actually is," Micki said. "A girl in fencing class at my boarding school tried to put my eye out because she thought I was messing with her boyfriend." Micki shrugged at the expression on their faces. "Some of those Italian girls get very emotional."

"And were you," Tobias asked.

"Was I what?"

"Messing with her boyfriend," Tobias said.

Micki shrugged. "I tried to tell her I liked older men, but she wouldn't listen. I wouldn't have gone out with her boyfriend on a bet."

Hattie led them around the building and into a side door. They followed her through a short, carpeted hallway to Hattie's private office. Her office was not neat. There were books and magazines piled up everywhere. Tobias and Micki had to clean off chairs to sit down. On a cluttered counter behind Hattie's desk there were dozens of arrowheads, photographs, pieces of what looked like farm equipment and even what looked like a small gasoline engine. On another table in the corner there was a microscope with slides scattered around.

And there was the spider.

45

The spider was hard to miss. It was in a huge aquarium on the floor, but the glass cage didn't look big enough to hold it. It scurried over to the side of the glass and looked as if it was pressing his face against to look at Tobias. Tobias wondered if it was hungry.

"Its main diet is wayward students," Hattie said, as if reading his mind. "I just gave it a freshman who was late on an assignment so he won't be hungry for a while."

"That's an incredibly big spider," Tobias said nervously.

"He's harmless except for really bad students," Hattie said, with a smile. "But you didn't come here to talk about my pet."

"No," Tobias said. "I came to talk to you about Kalanu."

"Which Kalanu?" Hattie asked. "That covers a lot of territory. Is this anything to do with the child that was kidnapped? I've been listening on the radio. It's a terrible thing."

"The man that kidnapped her claimed that Kalanu took her," Tobias said, "The spirit of the mountain."

Hattie sighed. "Another of your grandfather's stories."

"I'm afraid so," Tobias admitted.

"I don't understand," Micki said. "What's Tobias's grandfather to do with this?"

"There are literally thousands of legends and myths connected to these mountains and to the name Kalanu," Hattie explained. "There was a Kalanu, who was a great Cherokee warrior and medicine chief who died somewhere on a hilltop in Ohio. Legend says he was the last man standing in a savage battle. But the name Kalanu has been given to others through the years. The name means Raven in Cherokee. In fact, there was a movement back in the early fifties to change the name of the county from Kalanu to Raven County, but it never happened."

"But what does that have to do with Tobias's grandfather?" Micki asked.

"Tobias's grandfather was a poet and musician and storyteller. For a long time he traveled all over the Appalachian area appearing at fairs and concerts and craft shows. He became quite famous for his mandolin music and for his ability to tell stories. Later, he wrote a book called 'Tales around a Smoky Mountain Campfire.' But that's kind of where the trouble started."

"What trouble?" Micki said.

"My grandfather took great liberties with the truth," Tobias said.

Hattie nodded her head. "It would be fair to say he was historically inaccurate and perhaps his most famous creation was his story of what happened to the old settlement on Kalanu, and of Kalanu, the witch, the spirit of the mountain."

"He made up the witch," Micki said.

"Not entirely," Hattie said. "Benjamin Atkins never made up things completely. He always used a blend of fact and fiction. There is actually a Cherokee witch called Kalanu Ahkyeliski. It means the Raven Mocker. The Raven Mockers are old witches who eat the hearts of the diseased and dying. Benjamin actually called his witch a Raven Mocker in a couple of places, but his witch in no way resembled the witches of Cherokee legend. His witch was big and powerful and young, a protector of the mountain, a man who could transform himself into a raven so that he could look fly over it. He used this witch to explain the desertion of the settlement of Old Kalanu. He said Kalanu drove the early settlers off."

"But did he kidnap little children?" Micki asked.

"Yes," Hattie said. "I'm afraid he did. Wait a moment. Let me fetch something from the other office."

Hattie left them. Tobias eyed the spider. It hadn't moved. It seemed to be staring at him.

"There's nothing really to worry about," Micki said. "There's never been a known human fatality from the bite of a tarantula."

"And you'd know this how?"

"I read a lot about them. I used to have one as a pet."

"Why am I not surprised?"" Tobias said. "I bet you're also fond of snakes."

"I don't mind them," Micki said.

Hattie returned with a book Tobias recognized. She put it into his lap. It was becoming a rare book. Tales around a Smoky Mountain Campfire first published in 1942, with one reprinting sometime in the fifties. There was a picture of his grandfather on the front, standing in front of his cabin on Mount Rawls. His

47

grandfather had passed away while he was in the Marines. He still missed him.

"Read the story, Tobias," Hattie suggested.

The story of Old Kalanu was the first story in the book. He had heard his grandfather tell it many times so many times that, as he started reading, he could not help but get into the same singsong rhythm his grandfather had used. It was a long story, full of beautiful descriptions of actual places on the mountain, places his grandfather had hiked and camped. There was no doubt that Benjamin Atkins had known the mountain.

There was silence for a moment as he closed the story.

"Wow," Micki said.

"Yes," Hattie said. "I think 'wow' is the right word. I always wished I could have heard Benjamin Atkins in person, but now, somehow I think I have."

"I'm not sure it helps us find Sharon, though," Tobias said. "I was hoping there would be mention of a Cloud Place. I couldn't remember it in his writings, but the Cloud Place is where Jessop said Kalanu took the child."

"I do not remember anything called a Cloud Place," Hattie said.

"But it sounds like Jessop either read the story or had somebody tell it to him," Micki said. "I mean, everything fits together. Your grandfather said the original witch kidnapped the children of the settlement and offered to return them unharmed if the settlers returned to the valley. In the story the children were set free."

"So this witch might require some sort of payment," Hattie said. "A ransom demand?"

"If the witch remains true to the story," Tobias said. "I've got to talk to Jessop again. I've got to find out who Kalanu is, and I've got to find the Cloud Place. Jessop is the only one who knows."

"And he's taken so many drugs, he can't remember his own name," Micki said.

"We could always threaten to feed him to the spider," Tobias said.

CHAPTER SEVEN

He normally liked a lot of different positions and making love to him was a little like running a marathon. Today it was quick and savage, almost as if he had been excited beyond control as soon as he walked through the door. He had torn her panties in the process of removing her clothes and it had been vanilla, missionary, with no concern for her. When he was done, he rolled off and stomped into the bathroom, stopping only for a moment to turn on the television. She lay behind the thin sheet listening to the hum of the cheap air conditioner in the window, only vaguely aware of the voices from the television. She heard the sound of the shower running, and she wondered once again what she was doing with Barry Silverman.

Honestly, she didn't like him much. He was a caricature. The outside was charming and good looking, but the inside was shallow. He had no real feelings for anyone. He was married with three children, but he had no pictures of his family, not even on his desk at work. She also knew that he collected women like other men collected watches or baseball cards, and he made no distinction at married or single. In fact, she thought he liked the excitement of being with a married woman. His wife was a tired, sad looking woman who spent a lot of time with charity work. She knew they did not sleep in the same bed anymore.

She knew he would never be capable of real love because there was nobody in the world he loved as much as himself.

A name from the lips of a television news person broken through her lethargy and she sat up quickly in the bed, holding the sheet up to her breasts. On the small television screen, she saw the attractive female reporter from Gainesville holding up a mike in front of two people. One of them was Matt Trueblood's daughter, and the other was her husband.

Seeing Tobias on television made her shiver. It was like looking at one of those pictures of the concentration camp survivors of World War II. Because he was so tall, it made it worse. Her first feeling was anger. His job had separated them from the beginning. It was a part of him she could not have. Then his injury and the long, dreary time of waiting for him to recover. And when he hadn't woken up in a long time, it was a time of waiting for him to die, a long, endless nightmare of waiting for a phone call in the middle of the night and rushing to the hospital to find he had somehow recovered again, heart beating normally, but still in the deep, dark sleep. The terrible silence of sitting with him in the evenings after work, as a good wife was supposed to do, listening to the sound of hi shallow breathing. A scream grew inside her, a terrible screeching sound that did not pass her lips, but reverberated night and day in her head.

At first she had prayed for his recovery and then she had prayed for his death.

And at her lowest point, Barry Silverman had come along.

Oh, she couldn't blame it all on him.

From the beginning, she knew what he wanted. She was another notch on his bedpost, especially sweet because of the animosity between the Silverman family and the Atkins family that went back nearly a hundred years. It seemed they were always on opposing sides, mostly because the Atkins were strong environmentalists who respected old culture and tradition, and the Silverman's were entrepreneurs, interested only in profit.

"I know you are really going through a lot," Barry Silverman had said, stopping by her office one morning at the bank. "Let me take you out to lunch today. It might help take your mind off things."

All the time she had felt his eyes on her, measuring her, probing for weakness as a hunter will do and Barry Silverman was definitely a hunter. She refused him the first couple of times, but he was insistent.

"Swede wouldn't mind," Barry said. "He would want you to relax and enjoy yourself a little. You need to unwind. You are so tense."

And finally she relented and afternoon lunches became quiet dinners in Atlanta, a slow, carefully planned seduction and when he finally tumbled her into bed, she went with only a token protest. He courted her for a while. He took her to weekend retreats in Atlanta. He bought her jewelry and lingerie and had her car repaired when it was acting funny. She always protested, but she always ended up accepting. He wore her down with his charm, his humor; his way of making her think she was the most important

50

person in the world to him. And all the time she knew he was only using her, but then she thought she was using him in the same way.

And Swede would never know. It would never hurt him because in her heart she knew he would never wake up. He was already dead for all practical purposes.

But then he did wake up and the sweet romantic retreats had become urgent afternoon meetings at different motels, thirty minutes of quick, mechanical passion that usually left her feeling tired and dispirited, and used … but she still hadn't broken it off.

And now the Trueblood girl had dragged Tobias up the mountain when he could barely walk.It wasn't right or fair. It would not be the Sheriff of Kalanu County or that damned woman who would sit up with Tobias half the night when he was sick, and his head pounding. It would not be Micki Trueblood, who would be holding his hand while he was throwing up.

She wanted to throw something at the television.

The shower stopped and Barry Silverman came out of the bathroom, drying himself off. She knew he did it on purpose. He was vain about his muscular physique. He had a personal trainer and he spent several hours a week at the gym. He was in good shape, no question, but sometimes it irritated her when he seemed to preen like a peacock. There were times he would stand in front of her and stretch like one of those muscle building freaks during a competition.

Today she felt no admiration for his muscles. She wanted to claw his eyes out.

"You knew about this," she said.

They were replaying the airport scene on the television. He looked at it and shrugged.

"It's no big deal. They wanted Swede to talk to the guy who kidnapped the girl, but it was a waste of time. Hell, he was acting like he was old buddies with the kidnapper. "

"You saw the Indian girl on the mountain, Micki Trueblood."

He shrugged.

"She's the one who got you all excited."

"You get me excited, baby," Barry said.

"You bastard," she said.

"Come on, baby," Silverman said. "It wasn't like that. I hardly spoke to the woman. You know you're the only woman I want."

"You're a liar. I'm just convenient."

She saw the cruel glint of humor in his eyes. He dropped the towel on the floor and started to dress. He was usually very meticulous with his clothing. He usually hung it carefully up before their sessions. Today he had torn off his guard uniform hurriedly and dropped everything on the floor. He looked unhappy with the wrinkles as he buckled his pants.

"I don't want to see you anymore," she said.

He shrugged. "Okay. I was getting a little weary of you anyway. The truth is you're not my type, Abby. I like my women with a little more life in them. You're just a romantic with a silly way of looking at the world. You weren't even a challenge. Your husband was in a coma and you were spreading your legs for me. What really excited me about you was that you were his wife and I hate him. So I screwed him a little by screwing you."

"You're a piece of trash," she said. She was trying not to cry but her words caught in her throat in a choking sob.

"You are calling me trash," he said. "Wasn't it just a week ago you were telling me how much you wanted to please me in the office after hours one night? Wasn't it you on your knees? I think you better take a long look at yourself before you start calling other people trash."

The tears came and she turned her head away from him and sobbed into her pillow while he finished dressing. She heard the door shut as he left. She got up and went into the bathroom and turned the shower on and stood under it for a half-hour, until the water got tepid. The hot water did not make her feel clean.

Naked, she walked back into the bedroom and sat on the corner of the bed. She picked up her purse off the floor and took out the small bottle of pills her doctor had given her to help her sleep. She looked at the bottle for a long time, considering, and then put the bottle back into her purse.

A moment later she rushed back into the bathroom and threw up her breakfast.

CHAPTER EIGHT

When Micki turned the jeep into the fenced-in parking area behind the Kalanu County jail, they were surprised to see a press conference going on. Sheriff Abercorn was wearing his uniform, which was unusual, and he stood on a raised wooden platform in front of a group of reporters. There was a news van from Atlanta parked near the street, and Tobias recognized a distinguished looking white-haired man as being with a cable news agency.

"I think something's happened," Tobias said.

"Maybe they found her," Micki said.

"No. Abercorn doesn't look happy."

"How can you tell? He always looks miserable to me."

Micki parked in the rear and they were careful to remain in the shadows as they walked around to the front again in time to hear Abercorn reading a prepared speech.

"An hour ago we received a phone call from an individual claiming to be involved in the kidnapping of Sharon Bishop. He had several ransom demands. At present we still believe that Jessop acted alone in the kidnapping, but we are widening the scope of our investigation."

"What is the kidnapper demanding?" A reporter asked.

"I am not going to discuss specifics," Abercorn said. "There will be more information available at a later time, but right now we are still in the preliminary part of our investigation."

"Who received the ransom demand?" the same reporter asked.

"That would be discussing specifics," Abercorn said drily.

"Surely the name of the person who received the phone call is not a secret," another reporter said.

"It wouldn't be if I told you," Abercorn said.

There was some muted laughter.

"You're really not telling us anything," the cable news network man complained.

"We don't really know anything," Abercorn said. "As I said earlier, our belief is still that Jessop acted alone. The rest is just guess work. You will get the information when we get it."

"Do you think the girl is still being held on the mountain?" the cable newsman asked.

"We believe so. We are still continuing the search. The National Guard and civilian volunteers have been on the mountain all night. The only change we are making is that we are increasing our manpower and pushing out the circumference of the search area. In the meantime, investigators will be looking into the phone call and the ransom demand."

"Is Swede Atkins part of the investigative team?" Tracie Clavier asked,

Tobias had already glimpsed her standing back in the crowd. It was unusual for her. She was usually at the front of everything, and her good looks made her stand out. But now everyone was looking at her, and he had the sense she'd waited for just the right moment to ask her question. Other reporters were sensing the tension in her question, and they were like sharks starting to swim toward the blood in the water.

"Investigator Atkins is on medical leave," Abercorn said slowly.

"But he was on the mountain," Tracie said. "He did talk to Jessop."

"Yes."

"Aren't you afraid that having him involved in any sort of investigation would do more harm than good? A little girl's life hangs in the balance here. You can't have someone stumbling around who can't remember his name sometimes."

There was viciousness in her words that surprised Tobias. He felt Micki tense and he put his hand on her arm.

"I repeat," Abercorn said. "Investigator Atkins is on medical leave and not involved in this investigation. We asked him if he would help us out by establishing a dialogue with Jessop. At the time we thought he might talk to Swede. He wouldn't, and didn't. That was the end of it."

"Colonel Silverman said that bringing Atkins into the investigation was bad judgment on your part. He said Atkins messed up the only opportunity that you have for getting the information from Jessop."

"Colonel Silverman is not a policeman," Abercorn said.

In the yard one of the reporters had glanced over toward Tobias and Tobias knew it was only going to be a few moments before he was recognized.

"We need to get inside," he said. "Before the herd comes after us."

"Some reporters need to be locked up," Micki said.

"Maybe she believes what she's saying," Tobias said, "and maybe she's right."

"She's not been right since the doctor slapped her on her skinny little butt," Micki said.

They slipped unobserved through the front doors into the reception area. Before his injury Tobias heard talk of the county building a new jail. He had even seen plans for it. It was going to be a very modern-looking building along the first stretch of highway cleared away by the Windfall Project. In the front of the building there would be a few holding rooms and a spacious break room. Through an electronic door and down a long hallway would be the actual cells, a series of cells built in a semi-circle around a wide exercise yard. There would be good lighting, a library and recreation room for the few prisoners kept long-term.

But Tobias actually preferred the old jail. It had a historic sense about it, and it felt comfortable to him. Twice the state had fined the county because of the current jail. At times it was overcrowded and there weren't a lot of amenities for long term guests. And the lighting was poor in the lower part of the building, which made a lot of the prisoners refer to it as the dungeon. Some claimed the jail was haunted with the ghosts of the thousands of men and women who had been locked up there, but Tobias had never seen any ghosts.

When Tobias woke up from his coma, the new jail was still just photographs on an architect's drawing board. There was no money. It was cheaper to pay the state fine than to break ground for a modern building. And there was no road because the Windfall Project was stalled.

The only thing really accomplished was that the land had been purchased. Tobias suspected the speedy purchase of the land had more to do with it being owned by a member of the Silverman family. There was definitely a conflict of interest in the sale, but nobody was squawking too loud. Between banking and real estate, the Silverman family wielded a lot of power in Kalanu.

The current jail had a small reception area at the entrance. There was a hallway which was blocked by an electronic door, controlled by whomever sat behind the desk. Usually, it was a desk sergeant, but today it was a tall, willowy woman with long dark red hair, intelligent green eyes, and a thin smile. Marie Williams was the administrative head of the Sheriff's department. It was her job to buy the office equipment, answer the Sheriff's phone, keep track of his schedule, and enter department data in a strange kind of data machine nobody else could figure out how to operate.

She was officially a lieutenant with the department, but she never wore a uniform and she had never gone to the police academy. Giving her an official title and rank was only a way of getting her paid higher than the salary a police clerk.

There was no doubt she had a fierce loyalty to the department and to the Sheriff. Her dedication to the job and her choice of plain, dark clothing and little makeup caused a lot of the officers to refer to her as the Nun, but none of them to her face.

"So Rip Van Winkle has returned," she said, looking up from a paper she was reading.

"I knew you would be sympathetic," Tobias said. "Are you now working the front desk too?"

"Sergeant Mathis is on the road," she said. "Except for the Sheriff and two deputies down in the jail, everybody is either on the road or up on the mountain."

"Has Owen brought Jessop down?"

"A half hour ago," she said.

She buzzed them through the large, heavy door. Through the door they entered a long, narrow hallway. The Nun came around the desk and stood looking at Tobias for a moment. Then, impulsively she put her arms around his neck and hugged him tightly. Tobias was shocked. In all the years of working with her, he had never known her to show emotion. When she drew back, there were tears in her eyes.

"You were missed," she said.

"I didn't even think you liked me," he said.

"You're better than some," she admitted.

She stood back and the emotional moment was gone. Her eyes were cold again, and the thin smile was back. "The Sheriff wants you to talk to Jessop again."

"What's going on?"

"The mother of Sharon Bishop received a phone call that has stirred up a hornet's nest."

"What was the demand?"

"That the Governor immediately make a promise that the Windfall Project would be stopped forever, that the land already purchased would be designated park land, and that all the building that had already been done would be removed and the land put back in its pristine state."

"The blackmailer actually said pristine."

"That's what the mother said."

"Kidnappers are getting a better vocabulary," Tobias said.

"Anyway, the Sheriff says you're probably right about Jessop having a partner. He says maybe you can try Jessop again and get something out of him. Owen talked to him a little, but he's pretty much shut down."

"Defense mechanism," Tobias said. "The less he says the less trouble he's likely to be in."

"He's already in a lot of trouble. A lot of people are talking about an old-fashioned lynching. Especially after that idiot Barry Silverman gave his interview to that woman reporter. He made it look like the Sheriff was incompetent, and that he was actually having to run the investigation and the search. I would like to string that man up by his ..." She stopped and took a deep breath.

Tobias was grinning.

"What?" She said.

"I just had a sudden mental image of you standing out front with a shotgun like Wyatt Earp trying to hold off a lynch mob."

She didn't look as if she appreciated the joke. She started to say something else but the phone rang and she hurried to answer it.

Tobias studied her for a moment. He had never seen the softness in her before. She kept it well hidden under her dull, drab clothes and her businesslike manner, but when she wasn't wearing the armor of the Nun, there was something very appealing about her. She looked up and caught his eye and all traces of softness disappeared.

"We've got Jessop in Interview One."

"Okay," he said.

He and Micki continued on down the hall to the interview rooms. They found Owen standing at the door to the first room on the right. The door was closed and he was sipping coffee from a Styrofoam cup.

"I don't have him cuffed," Owen said. "I offered him coffee, water, or soft drinks, but he didn't answer. He hasn't spoken to anyone since he spoke to you up on the mountain. He starts humming, sometimes."

"Humming?" Tobias asked.

"Yeah. It's a familiar tune, but I can't place it. I think it's some show tune. Anyway, he hummed it all the way down the mountain. I'm glad I don't have to listen anymore. I wish you luck. If you would, call the Nun at the desk when you're done and have her bring up one of the guys from the dungeon to take him down. I have to get back on the road. I've got three burglaries and an assault, and it's not even a full moon."

"Thanks, Owen," Tobias said.

"What's that about a full moon?" Micki asked, as Owen left them.

"It's an old police legend, or maybe it's fact, I don't know. I think people have done research. But it's said that people commit more crimes when there's a full moon.'

"Really?" Micki asked.

"There are more things in heaven and earth, Horatio," Tobias said.

"Shakespeare now," Micki said. "You are full of surprises."

'You don't know the half of it," Tobias said.

Jessop had been cleaned up. He had showered and he was bandaged. He wore a bright orange jail uniform. He did not look at them. His hands were on the table and he was rocking. He was humming. Tobias recognized the tune immediately. It was an old hymn, Rock of Ages.

"How do you feel, Clyde?" Tobias asked.

Clyde looked at them, and his eyes focused.

"I didn't hurt that girl," he said.

The drugs and alcohol were wearing off. The pupils of his eyes were almost back to normal.

"So where is she, Clyde?"

"I told you already. Kalanu took her."

"That's what you said, all right. You said Kalanu turned into a raven and picked her up and took her up to the Cloud Place. So where is the Cloud Place?"

"His place on the mountain," Clyde said.

"Where exactly is that?"

Clyde shook his head. "Nobody knows."

"You're not being a lot of help, Clyde. You said you didn't want to hurt the girl. You said you wanted to be her friend."

"That's all I wanted," he said.

"But now she's up there on that mountain and she's cold and she's hungry and she's cared. If you want to be her friend, tell me where she is."

"I've told you over and over," Clyde Jessop said. "She's with Kalanu. He's got her."

"Who is Kalanu, Clyde?'

Clyde Jessop looked as if he didn't understand the question. He shrugged. "He's the spirit of the mountain. He's the witch."

"There are no such things as witches," Tobias said.

"Your grandfather believed," Clyde Jessop insisted.

"My grandfather made up things sometimes. I told you that. He liked to tell stories, but that's all they were. Just stories. Now we believe somebody helped you to kidnap that little girl. A person and not some sort of witch-bird. So who was this person, Jessop?"

"Kalanu," Clyde Jessop insisted.

Tobias closed his eyes. His headache was back. He needed one of those little pills that the doctor had given him, but the problem with those pills was that everything grew out of focus. But at the moment, everything was hurting. Every time he moved, it was like fiery-hot needles were piercing his flesh. He tried to keep the irritation out of his voice. He even tried to smile. He didn't think it worked very well. Clyde Jessop drew back in his chair as if he had caught a glimpse of something ugly in Tobias's face.

"I know that Kalanu is a real man, Clyde," Tobias said. "It's someone you know, and I want you to give me his name."

"He's always been Kalanu," Clyde said.

"You're lying, Clyde," Tobias said. "Who is he? Was he someone you met in jail? Was he someone you met at the Baptist place? Was he someone you knew from Gainesville, from your past? Who is he, Clyde?"

"He's the protector of the mountain," Clyde said.

"You think he's going to rescue you? You think he's going to protect you this time when you go to jail. Think again, Clyde. They're going to put you back in prison and this time it's going to be a lot worse. You tell us his name and maybe we can keep you out of the general population. Maybe we can send you someplace where they don't know you're a child molester and that you kidnap little girls."

Clyde Jessop got a little pale. "He's always been Kalanu."

"No. And you know he's just a man."

"No."

"So if he's Kalanu, why didn't he come up with a better plan? Why did he have to use you to get the girl? Or maybe he did give you a better plan? Maybe he told you to wait until it was really dark and everybody was asleep. But you got impatient, didn't you? You wanted to get your hands on her."

"No."

"You messed it up, didn't you? He told you what to do, but you messed it up."

"I did what he told me," Clyde Jessop insisted.

"Did you start getting those old feelings? You couldn't make yourself wait. You saw her in her pajamas and you broke in while everybody was still awake. And you were seen. Surely Kalanu didn't want it that way."

"I needed to talk to her," Clyde said.

He licked his lips and Tobias felt a wave of revulsion. He hoped he kept it hidden under a strict poker face, but it was becoming hard not to let his real feelings show.

He felt as if it had been another lifetime since he had dealt with people like Jessop.

"I just wanted to talk to her," Clyde repeated. "Just talk to her. That's all."

"The man who has her is not your friend, Clyde," Tobias said. "He's left you in here without helping you. If he were truly Kalanu, he would have taken you out of his jail by now. He's just a man. He's just a crazy man and you need to tell us his name."

For a few moments Clyde Jessop showed a fearful intelligence in his eyes, the sudden animal-like realization that he was trapped. For a few moments he knew Tobias was telling the truth. He glanced nervously around as if he expected the raven to carry him away. But then Tobias saw Jessop blink the truth away and retreat back into the shallow world of his fantasy. Jessop leaned back and closed his eyes and Tobias inwardly cursed because he knew had gotten all the information he was going to get. Jessop was retreating to the deepest part of his mind, closing the doors, becoming almost cationic.

"I wasn't going to hurt her," he said. "She was so pretty. So fragile. I just wanted to talk to her, to be her friend. I don't have friends. I wanted to be her friend. I wouldn't have hurt her. I would never hurt any of those children."

Without looking at her, Tobias sensed Micki's tension. He knew it would take little provocation for her to come across the table after Jessop.

"Sure, you were, Clyde," Tobias said. "It's what you do. You hurt little children because you were hurt yourself. You are so full of hate and bitterness and need that you can't help but hurt them. It makes you feel more like a man. It's a sickness, but it's who you are. Of course you were going to hurt her."

Clyde opened his eyes.

'I'm not talking to you anymore."

"That's too damn bad. "You've been a fountain of information so far."

CHAPTER NINE

In the hallway outside the holding cell, a short, squat man with a wide grin and a balding head leaned against the wall. He gave Micki a thorough inspection and Tobias felt her body tense up.

"Is this your new partner, Swede?" he asked.

"I've seen that look in your eyes before and I would be very careful what you say from this point on," Tobias said. "This is Micki Trueblood and she's sort of sensitive and she has a very short fuse. I would recommend keeping my distance and being respectful at all times."

"Sorry, Mam," he said. "I will be on my best behavior."

"This gentleman's name is Mitchell Carp, like the fish," Tobias said. "He works for the Governor. I've never been sure doing exactly what. He used to be one of the proud and the few and then he worked for an honest living as a patrol officer with DeKalb County. Now he's some sort of special investigator."

"You two are friends," Micki said.

"I wouldn't go that far," Mitchell said, "but us old Marines have to stick together. You got some time for some coffee, Swede?"

"Coffee is always good."

They were by themselves in the break room. Mitchell Carp volunteered to buy the coffee from the vending machine, and he couldn't help but give Micki another long look as he put her cup down in front of her.

"Careful, boy," Tobias said. "I'm telling you that she's not domesticated."

"Can't help it," he said. "You are one gorgeous lady, Micki. And you remind me of somebody. I can't quite figure it out."

"The actress, Imelda Magliano," Tobias said.

62

Mitchell's eyes grew wider.

"The Italian Brigitte Bardot. Incredible. There's an odd contrast with the obvious Native American in your blood, but those are her eyes."

"My mother was not famous for her eyes," Micki said.

Carp involuntarily glanced down at Micki's chest for a moment and then jerked his head back up, Micki was smiling, but there was little warmth in her eyes.

"Imelda Magliano was your mother?" Carp asked.

"Pull your tongue back in, Carp," Tobias said. "You're going to trip over it."

Tobias had known Mitchell Carp for many years. Mitchell was a good investigator, another man who had seen it all from the jungles of Vietnam to the blinking neon lights of the worst part of town. Tobias had not thought it possible for Mitchell to be stunned by anything, but he looked stunned now. He looked up and caught Tobias grinning, and he looked embarrassed.

"You didn't buy me coffee to drool all over Micki," Tobias said. "What is it you want, Mitchell?"

Mitchell sipped his coffee. "I figure you know. You heard outside. Somebody's made a phone call saying the girl will be returned unharmed if the governor agrees to permanently shut down the Windfall Project. The Governor loves the Windfall Project and this is incredibly bad timing."

"Yeah, the child should have picked a better time to be kidnapped."

"Come on, Swede," Mitchell said. "You know that's not what I meant."

"Yeah, I know," Tobias said. "Sorry. So will the Governor consider shutting it down for good?"

"Not going to happen," Mitchell said. "But on the other hand, it's a political landmine if something does happen to that child."

"Why is there such strong opposition to it?" Tobias asked. "I remember there were a few voices raised in protest before I did my Rip Van Winkle act, but it looks to have gotten worse."

"People need causes, I guess," Mitchell said. "People need things to fuss about or worry over. I expect there are really a few

63

people out there who believe the project would hurt the environment, but the rest are followers."

"Is money involved?"

Mitchell shook his head. "Not in the way you think. Nobody stands to make a profit or if they do, it's generic. It's the profit that the stores or shops might get because of increased tourist pressure. But we're not talking about big money. And I don't see how anybody would lose anything. It's mostly government land. It belongs to the forest service. So there doesn't seem to be any monetary reason for being in opposition. Believe me, I've asked myself the same questions you're asking and I couldn't find a thing. There's no political maneuvering behind the scenes. Everything is right out in the open."

"And you think they're going to start the project back up?"

Mitchell looked a little uncomfortable but then he grinned. "Hell, you already figured that out because I'm here."

"Who else would know?"

"There's a lot of private funding involved from big corporations and some state money and some money from Kalanu County and a few surrounding areas. Even the college is giving an endowment so I suppose a lot of people would know."

"So maybe it's got nothing to do with the kidnapping," Tobias suggested. "Maybe it's just somebody taking advantage of a really bad situation."

"That's what I'm here for," Mitchell said. "The Governor wants me to hang around and give him all the information I can."

"And how much information have you given him so far?" Tobias asked.

"Absolutely zip."

"Pretty much what I've got also," Tobias said.

.....

Sheriff Harvey Abercorn was in his office. He sat behind his battered desk with his feet propped up and his shoes off. There was a small hole in the middle of one of his thick wool socks. He looked tired and sore and he did not look happy to see them. He took his feet off his desk and sat up.

"So what is it?" Harvey asked. "And why do I have the feeling I'm not going to like it?"

"We need to find out everybody Clyde Jessop has ever been in jail with."

"Is that all?"

"And we need to find out if anybody Jessop was in jail with is from this area, or has any connection to my grandfather or to Windfall."

Harvey rubbed his eyes. "Do you have any idea what the general prison population is in the state of Georgia?"

"No," Tobias admitted.

"Neither do I, but based on the amount of criminal cases we make in Kalanu County alone, I expect there's a huge number. There are a ton of city and county jails and work camps and Clyde Jessop has been in and out of jail since he was thirteen and able to see over the steering wheel enough to steal his first car."

"I know it'll be a tough task," Tobias said.

"Not tough. Impossible."

'That's why I want to use Eddie Syler."

"Who's Eddie Slyer?" Micki asked.

Harvey groaned. "I'm going to pretend I didn't hear that."

"Who's Eddie Slyer?" Micki asked again.

"He's a computer genius," Tobias said.

"He's a thief," Harvey Abercorn said.

"We need him," Tobias insisted.

"I don't want him involved with this department in any shape or fashion He should have been locked up the last time instead of some bleeding heart probation. He nearly destroyed the banking institution in the state of Georgia.

"That's an exaggeration," Tobias said.

"No way," Harvey said.

"Not even with the Governor's pardon?" Carp asked.

Harvey turned his head and glared at Carp. "You stay out of this. You're nothing but the Governor's flunky."

"Those are harsh words," Carp said.

"But true," Harvey insisted. "And besides, you know the odds are against Sharon Bishop still being alive.

"But do we take that chance, Harvey?" Tobias said. "Do we just give up, or do we try everything we can? I admit it's a risk. He is not like other people. There may be other people who can help, but we'd have to find them on short notice and it would take them longer. I just have a feeling that we don't have that kind of time. Eddie can do it in the blink of an eye. He's a genius."

"A strange, warped genius and we're all going to jail. You, me, Carp and the Governor. Probably Micki will get a mistrial because she's pretty."

"Thank you," Micki said.

"But the rest of us are going to end up eating prison food."

"We need somebody who can cut through the red tape," Carp insisted.

"You mean someone who can illegally hack programs," Harvey said. "This gets better and better. I don't want him anywhere near the station."

"No," Tobias said.

"The good Lord help us if the reporters find out," Harvey said. Harvey laced his hands behind his head and leaned back up in his swivel chair. For a long time nobody moved or said anything. Sheriff Harvey Abercorn continued to stare up at the ceiling.

"What are you doing, Sheriff," Micki finally asked.

"Searching for the sword of Damocles," Harvey said.

CHAPTER TEN

Eddie Tyler lived in the picturesque little town of Helen, Georgia. Back in the sixties Helen had been a dying logging town, but enterprising businessmen had gotten the idea of turning the town into an exact replica of a Bavarian Village in the Alps. It had worked. The tourists had flocked to the city and now the area boasted of hiking trails, river rafting, cozy little Alpine Chalets for honeymooners, and a main street full of shops with clothing, art, candy and gifts.

Eddie lived in an apartment above a restaurant just beyond the Chattahoochee River. There were few tourists around on such a cold, dreary day. A lot of the shops were closed. The place had the look of an amusement park after the crowds had gone home. Micki parked in the street in front of the restaurant.

"What are we waiting for?" Micki asked

"We're waiting for Eddie's lawyer," Tobias said. "She said she'd be here as quick as she could."

Micki glanced up at the sign above the restaurant.

"The Wurst Restaurant," she said.

"Sausage," Tobias explained. "The restaurant is famous for different kinds of sausage. "

Tobias was nervous with impatience. He felt like he was getting closer to the answers and he kept thinking of how long the little girl had been on the mountain. He wanted to be doing something. He couldn't think of what else to do.

"Why are we waiting for the lawyer?" Micki said.

"We have to be careful with Eddie," Tobias said. "There is more than a legal problem involved here. You see, Eddie is an idiot savant. Sometimes he doesn't know what's good for him. His lawyer is sort of his business manager, friend and legal advisor. I'd prefer having her present."

"I see," Micki said. "You like this kid, don't you?"

"He's a good kid," Tobias said. "He has a good heart."

"So why is he in Harvey Abercorn's black book," Micki said.

67

"Harvey is scared of him. So am I. We all should be."

"Why?"

"Because all of our lives are contained in little boxes accessible to anyone who can hack in and look. Once upon a time information was held in metal cabinets. If you went for a car loan, all the papers were filed in the office. Now they are filed on the internet. Births, marriages, divorces, court dates, social security numbers, everything that makes us who we are. And all of it is available if you know where to look. Eddie Syler has a talent for being able to find that kind of information as easily as other people opening a book."

"So he's a computer hacker," Micki said.

"He's far more complicated than that. Think of the smartest person you know, or the most talented or the most athletic. These people were born with special skills that make them better at what they do than anyone else, and yet somewhere along the line somebody had to teach them. A brilliant concert pianist doesn't just sit down at the piano and play a concerto the first time he sees the keys. He had to learn music. He has to practice. Eddie never had to practice. One day he sat down at a computer and just knew what to do. It's almost as if he has some sort of alien symbiosis with the computer. It gives him an uncanny ability to hack into the most secure web site incredibly fast, almost as if he sees the password in his head. It also, unfortunately, made him an incredibly gifted thief."

"So why is he not in jail somewhere?" Micki asked.

Tobias sighed. "Let me tell you a little about his history. He grew up here. His mother came to work here as a waitress with Eddie was a baby. It's rumored she became the mistress of the man who owned the restaurant, a fellow named Nobles. What is not rumor is that when Nobles died, he had no other family and he left the restaurant to her. Nobody ever knew Eddie's father, but he was a troubled kid. At times he was violent. His mother was a hard woman. She refused to send Eddie to the kind of schools that might help him. She said there wasn't anything wrong with him. There was a lot of back and forth and in the end Eddie didn't go to school very much."

"How sad," Micki said.

"But it was discovered that he could do things other people couldn't do. He could add figures in his head. He could remember passages of books verbatim after reading it once. He learned to play the piano by watching and listening to other people play. And then he got interested in computers. He was fascinated by them. And people around here found he could figure out what was wrong with them if their home computer went bad. And when he gave their computers back to them, somehow the software always ran better and faster and more cleanly. Then about ten years ago Eddie went into partnership with an Atlanta company after he designed a cheap, very functional computer. It sold well and Eddie made quite a profit from it."

"So how did he become a thief?"

"He's like a child, really. There's a kind of innocence about him. Eddie never really grasped the concept of money. His mother was shrewd enough to find Eddie a very business manager slash lawyer who handles all his financial needs. He owns the restaurant, but the manager does the hiring and firing, and makes his investments. He gives Eddie an allowance to live on."

"But you're still not telling me how he became a thief."

"It's a gray area. There are things I'm not supposed to discuss."

"So tell me anyway. "

"Eddie moved money around. He didn't think there was anything wrong with it. I guess maybe you'd call him a socialist because he took money from the wealthy and gave it to those in need."

"Kind of a modern day Robin Hood," Micki said.

"Yes. And the people he took it from usually didn't complain."

"Why not?"

"Because of how they had gotten the money in the first place and they didn't like the idea of having a lot of prying investigator's eyes looking at their finances.'

"He was stealing from other thieves."

Tobias nodded. "Thieves and drug pushers and mostly every kind of thief imaginable."

"And he'd been doing it for a long time."

"Several years before I caught him," Tobias said.

"How?"

"This is the gray area I'm not supposed to talk about. There were a lot of lawyers and politicians involved. "

"You can't leave me hanging," Micki said.

Tobias thought for a moment and then nodded his head. "Oh hell, it probably doesn't matter now anyway as we're about to reopen this particular can of worms. There was a company. Call it company X. Company X was a fairly profitable company. It was so profitable that it came to the attention of a certain businessman. He wanted to buy the company, but the owner wouldn't sell. So he applied pressure. The owner still wouldn't sell. He applied more pressure. The rich man had friends in politics. He had a friend who was a judge. Somehow between them they found a way to force the owner to sell. Then the businessman and the judge and a few politicians sold the business in pieces and took the profits without a backward look. People were put out of work. The owner killed himself.'

"That's horrible," Micki said.

"But it was perfectly legal. And the owner was a friend of Eddie's. So Eddie took the money back and he gave it to the families. But however unethical they might have been, they did nothing illegal. And the honest citizens went screaming for the cops. And I was the chosen one sent to retrieve the money"

"And you caught him," she said.

"Yes. It wasn't easy and I had to have a lot of help. I ended up using about a dozen of the FBI's best computer guys and they still had trouble following the path, but eventually it led to Eddie. It was kind of funny, in a way. We thought we were faced with a mob of computer hackers. We showed up at the restaurant in the middle of the night, swat team and all. Busted the door down and found Eddie sitting on the couch in his underwear watching an old beach movie from the sixties. He never denied doing any of it. I called his lawyer down myself, the one his mother had left in charge. The lawyer tried to get Eddie to stop talking but he wouldn't. It was a mess. This had been going on since Eddie was sixteen. Harvey wasn't far off in his statement that Eddie could have sent the banking system in the state of Georgia into a tailspin."

"So why isn't he in jail?"

"It's the information age. All that talking Eddie did. A lot of it had to do with names and addresses. One of the addresses was the judge's young mistress in Atlanta, a gambling problem a state senator had, and so on and so forth. It didn't take an idiot to see his lawyer was going to use all those things and it was probably going to turn out to be one of those explosive trials ever to take place in our old courthouse.

"So they made a deal?'

"Yes. Eddie had to stay away from computers and leave other people's money alone and he wouldn't have to go to jail. It would have been no sense in locking him up. He didn't see what all the fuss was about. It was only money.'

"Only money?" Micki echoed.

"Yes. I think his lawyer's here. Her name is Margaret Bailey but people call her Peg. Don't be fooled by her grunge look. She's very sharp."

A battered old Volkswagen bug pulled in front of them, and a petite young woman got out of the driver's side. She was slightly plump, with reddish hair and pale skin. She had a small gold ring in her nose and a small tattoo of a rose visible on her neck. She came around to Tobias's side of the car and opened the door for him.

"Do you have it?" Peg asked, with a trace of belligerence in her voice.

Tobias took a folded envelope from his shirt pocket. She opened it and read it through twice without saying a word. She glanced up only one and that was when Micki walked around the car to the sidewalk. Her attention quickly went back to the document she held.

She finally pursed her lips and looked up at Tobias. "You understand that I don't really care a damn about this document. If you do anything to hurt Eddie in any way, I'm going to drag you and the Sheriff and the every member of your county commission, and the Governor into court and I'm going to keep every one of you so busy answering law suits for the rest of your life, you won't

71

have time to worry about anything else." She got closer to Tobias and arched her neck to look up at it. "I don't care that you're some kind of hero cop or that you're a crippled old man. I will drag you into court and make the rest of your life miserable."

"You've got to do something about your anger conflicts," Tobias said.

"I'm serious, Swede."

"I know you are, Peg. And you know I wouldn't do anything to hurt Eddie. But I really do need his help. There's a little girl up on the mountain and we need information quickly."

"You've got an entire state full of computer gurus," she said. "Why pick on Eddie?"

"That's exactly what the Sheriff said, "Tobias said. "And my answer to you is the same I gave to him. I need Eddie. He's got a talent nobody else does and we're running out of time. It's no big deal. I just need information."

"And he will have to hack into places to get it," she said. "Maybe."

"You heard what I said, Swede. Don't hurt him."

"I wouldn't do that," he said.

The young woman seemed to relax a little and she acknowledged Micki by holding out her hand. "I'm Margaret Jones. Most people call me Peg. I know who you are, of course. Everybody in four counties talks about you."

"I guess it's nice to be noticed," Micki said.

Peg smiled. "I'm sorry to come on so strong, but Eddie is very special to me. He was my father's client first, but Eddie and I went to grammar school together."

"I understand," Micki said.

"I'm not sure you do. Did you ever see the movie Forrest Gump?"

"Hasn't everyone?" Micki said.

"Eddie is Forrest Gump," Peg said.

.....

A few snow flurries fell as the three of them walked up the red oak stairway to Eddie's apartment. Tobias heard music playing and recognized it as one of the Beatles earlier songs. Eddie opened the door before they got there. Eddie was tall and slim, with dark blond hair almost to his shoulders. He had very bright blue eyes. He looked genuinely glad to see his lawyer. He looked a little less happy to see Tobias.

"Eddie, you remember investigator Tobias Atkins with the Sheriff's department and this is Micki Trueblood," Peg said. "They've come to ask your help."

"The cop," Eddie said.

'Yes,' Tobias said, "the cop."

"You took my computers away," Eddie said accusingly.

"He didn't take your computers away," Peg gently reminded him. "You were doing bad things with them."

"I don't want to talk to him," Eddie said

"Then talk to me," Peg insisted. "Let me in, Eddie."

He stepped aside for her, but then immediately shut the door in their faces. Tobias shivered a little as a cold blast of wind swept across the metal stairway where they stood. Micki wore only a light jacket, but she didn't seem bothered by the cold.

The music changed again. It was the Mommas and the Poppas and they were "California dreaming."

"I sense a pattern here," Micki said.

"His mother was a lot of things. A rude, hard woman who had little use of anyone, a sharp businesswoman, and if the rumors are to believed, a woman who wasn't above using her feminine charms to get what she wanted. How she came to Georgia, I'll never know, but she was originally from California. And she was a flower child right out of the sixties. Her choice of clothing, her music, her language, was all right off a street corner in Height-Asbury. She passed on her love of things sixties to Eddie."

Eddie opened the door again. He still did not look happy, but he let them in. The inside of the apartment was clean and neat enough for a Marine inspection. It looked as if it was a display model rather than an apartment somebody lived in. Eddie could not stand clutter.

On the far walls were dozens of old movie posters in glass frames on the wall. Most of the posters were collectibles Eddie had gotten off eBay, and most were of beach movies from the sixties. There were also several glass cases with memorabilia inside, also from the sixties.

Micki examined the large glass cases, and at the last one, she stopped. Inside the case was a miniature portrait of a gorgeous young woman in a blue dress. She wore pearls and long white gloves and dangling earrings. Her smile was angelic. There were other pictures of the same young woman in the case, along with an autographed book, an autographed comic, and two other photos that were autographed. In the bottom of the case there were several small teddy bears in different outfits, some autographed. Micki looked back at the oil painting in the middle.

"An Italian Madonna," Micki said.

At her elbow, Eddie spoke. It startled her. She had never heard his steps or sensed his presence, which was unusual for her.

"Peg said she went to live with the angels," Eddie said.

"Yes," Micki said. "I know."

"It was good she died."

"Good?" Micki asked.

"Peg explained. She said things die. People die. It's the way it's supposed to be. Sometimes when a person is hurting really bad, God takes them away to be with the angels. That's what happened to her. She went to be with the angels."

"I expect you're right, Eddie," Micki said.

"My Momma hurt badly and God took her away," Eddie said.

"I'm sorry, Eddie," Micki said.

Eddie shook his head. "I don't think Momma is with the angels, though."

Tobias cleared his throat. "Eddie, we need your help. There's a little girl who is in trouble on the mountain. We think a man has her, and you might be able to tell us who that man is."

"No," Eddie said.

"Yes," Tobias said. "We need information, Eddie, and we need it quickly. It's the only way to help that little girl and I know you want to help her. You've always helped people, Eddie."

74

He shook his head. "But I did bad things. And they won't let me have computers anymore."

"You have permission, Eddie," Peg said quickly. "The Governor of the state of Georgia says you've been punished enough and you can have your computers back. You can't do bad things with them anymore, only good things."

Eddie shook his head again. "I can't have computers. They said they would put me in jail."

Micki opened the glass case and she took down the small portrait. She held it up to Eddie's eyes. "I think she would want you to do this, Eddie. In fact, I know she would. She was a very gentle and caring person."

"You sound like you knew her," Eddie said.

"I knew her, Eddie," she said. "We were actually very distant cousins."

Eddie looked at the portrait to Micki and back again, his eyes widening in shock. The music changed again. This time it was Frankie Avalon singing Venus.

"Cousins," Eddie said.

"Very distant. But I know she would have wanted you to help this child if you could."

"I don't have my computers anymore,' Eddie said. "They took them all away."

"I know where they are," Peg said.

…..

The basement of the law office was small and cramped and filled with boxes. It was also filled with computers, at least a dozen of them. It took time to move them all upstairs and Eddie insisted they bring them all up. Tobias grew irritable, but Eddie had to have all the computers line up in a way only he understood. Fortunately, after a few years of not being used, they all hummed when Eddie turned them.

Tobias had never actually seen Eddie work at a computer before and the first thing that surprised him was that it was not Microsoft. When the computers turned on, they looked more like the old Atari games he remembered. It looked more like DOS programs. No fancy bells and whistles.

On the ride over, Tobias had explained exactly what they needed. Eddie did not seem to be listening. He started at Micki for the entire trip.

"I'll have to give you our password for our internet connection," Peg said. "It's not something you can write down. I have a key fob and you have to put it into the machine and let it read the password. It's all electronic."

Eddie was not listening, at least not to human voices. He had his head cocked as if he was actually listening to the computers and his fingers were flying on the keyboards. In a few seconds it was obvious he was connected to the internet, somehow bypassing the security codes in place.

"That's really scary," Peg said. "We paid a fortune for a secure connection."

Eddie still wasn't listening. His fingers moved rapidly. On one side of Eddie was a computer that looked like one of the old DOS computers Tobias had used back what seemed like a hundred years ago. It took him a moment to realize that Eddie was typing in programs that were appearing on the greenish screen. And the other two computers that were turned on did not have the familiar Microsoft programs Tobias was used to seeing. On these the screens kept changing rapidly. Tobias did notice a warning pop up that Eddie needed to enter his security clearance for a federal website, but the warning passed so quickly that Tobias wasn't even sure he'd seen it.

He told himself the brief glimpse was only a figment of his imagination.

Papers began to print on the nearby printer. Tobias picked up a handful of them and saw it was a list of names associated with Clyde Jessop. Somehow, in just a few moments, Eddie had written a program that took the name Clyde Jessop, and associated it with names from the five county area around Kalanu Mountain. Now the program was evidently running through every prison and jail in the state of Georgia. Papers kept printing out. By the time the computer stopped humming, there was a stack of papers as thick as a new novel.

It had taken Eddie no more than fifteen minutes in all.

They sat at a table across the street from the law office in a small pastry shop. The coffee was really good. It tasted a little like the apple Crunches they were eating. Each of them had a thick file of papers.

"This could take a while," Micki said.

"Concentrate on the odd ones," Tobias said. "See, if you can find child molesters or sex offenders in the group. Separate those. And anybody who is actually from Kalanu County. I asked Eddie to see if could narrow the field down a little, but in the meantime we've got these."

"You're right that Eddie is a bit odd," Micki said. "But he seems to manage pretty well and he's not a bad looking young man. Why doesn't he have a real girlfriend? I mean, uh, it's nice having a crush on a pretty girl on television and the movies, but real life girls are better.'"

"Because of his mother," Tobias said. "He shies away from girls."

"What's that got to do with his mother?"

"His mother told him he couldn't have a girlfriend because his children would be like him."

"You are kidding," Micki said. "That's sick. How could a mother do that to her child?"

"I don't know," Tobias said. "I can only imagine how tough it was with Eddie when he was a youngster. He would have all the same urges and she would have to have been very careful with him. Plus he was smarter than the average kid in a lot of ways, and probably frustrated with his inability to cope socially and the fact that he was different. It would have been tough."

"She still should have been horsewhipped saying a thing like that," Micki said.

Tobias only shrugged.

They sipped their coffee and ate crunches and read the papers, skimmed them really as they tried to find some connection between Clyde Jessop and Sharon Bishop, and some name that would jump out of them.

"Here's one that's kind of interesting," Tobias said. "A guy who was in Reidsville with Jessop. They shared a cell together.

According to this, he's working at a supermarket in Gainesville now and reporting to his probation officer on a regular basis."

Peg joined them with some more papers. Micki groaned.

"We're going to have to have help, Swede. It would take us months to get through all of this."

"I know," Tobias said. "I just keep hoping a name will jump out at us."

"Well, if it will encourage you," Peg said. "I think this is all, When I left, Eddie was playing some sort of computer game. I haven't seen him this happy in a while."

"You like him, don't you," Micki said.

"Yes," Peg said. "I do. But he doesn't see me as a woman. Just as a lawyer."

Micki nodded. She looked down at the papers as she raised her coffee cup to her lips. She never made it. A startled yelp came from her throat and both Tobias and Peg looked at her as if she had lost her mind.

"That name just jumped out at me," Micki yelped. "And it's one you're not going to like."

"Oh," Tobias said.

"Augustus Creel," she said.

A shiver went down his spine. He felt again the solid crunch of the shovel against his head, and sliding into unconsciousness. His life had changed forever in that moment. There were things he would never get back. "Gus Creel," Micki said, and he felt the darkness creeping up on him again.

"Creel was with Jessop in Reidsville?"

"For his last year," Micki said, reading the dates.

"The same time as the clerk in Gainesville. We need to talk to him."

"We can make it the next stop," Micki said.

They finished off their crunches and coffee and gathered up their papers. On the street Peg hugged Tobias.

"I've always liked you, Swede," Peg said. "But I swear to you that if this turns out badly for Eddie, I will personally hunt you down and I'll bring my own shovel."

"Just tell him not to steal," Tobias said.

78

"I'll tell him," Peg said, but there was a doubtful note in her voice.

In the car as Micki drove away from the law offices and back through Helen, across the long bridge over the Chattahoochee River, Tobias was thinking of Gus Creel. It still made no sense to him. He knew Creel well, had arrested him several times during the years. Creel was mean when he drank, and he liked the ladies but he was no child molester. The pattern didn't make sense.

"Gus Creel still might not be the one we're looking for." Micki suggested.

"It's him,' Tobias said. "I hate it, but I know it's him. And it doesn't make sense. He's not a child molester. He's a big dumb redneck who has been in one kind of trouble or another all of his life but none of it had anything to do with children or sex. But it's him.'

"How can you know for sure?"

"Because I don't want it to be him.

"Now that really makes sense," Micki said.

Patterns, Tobias thought. It was always about the patterns. No matter how the facts got twisted, the patterns would eventually fit together and make sense. But he couldn't seem to focus and the same dull headache kept him from concentrating as hard as he wished.

"Where would he go on the mountain," Tobias said. "Where is a Cloud Place?"

"Someplace up high," Micki said.

"It could be. Someplace in the clouds. Which would imply that he's at the very top of the mountain? Or it could be some variation of a Cherokee word that I'm not seeing. Like Kala Wind was originally some form of Cherokee word meaning winter or wind, but we've adapted it to our purpose. Sometimes the first settlers would hear the words and not be able to pronounce it, and they would use their own version. So Cloud Place might be anywhere or anything. It might not have anything to do with clouds. I know there is something I'm not remembering, something my grandfather might have told me."

"But Hattie couldn't remember it either," Micki reminded him. "Maybe Clyde Jessop heard it wrong, or he just made it up."

"Maybe he's made everything up," Tobias said bitterly. "Maybe we're on a wild goose chase and there's nothing up there but a broken child lying in a ravine somewhere."

"It's like you told Harvey," Micki said. "We have to keep trying."

He leaned his head back. His head still hurt but even more frustrating was his sense that there was something he could not see just beyond the edge of his consciousness. His mother's patterns all over again. He knew the cloud place was in the center of the quilt but he just couldn't' see it.

"You think Eddie will get into trouble again?" Micki asked. Her voice sounded far off.

"I think so. I hope it's not bad. I know that Peg will watch out over him, but he just doesn't think like other people."

"I hope he does okay,' Micki said.

"You liked him too?"

"Yes. There's sweetness about him."

"Well, you got him to help him. That was an inspiration that bit about being her cousin."

"I am her cousin. Very distant, but we are related."

Tobias opened his eyes and sat up straight in the seat. "You're telling the truth. You're Annette Fun cello's cousin?"

Micki looked amused. "Yes. It sounds as if you also had a crush on her.'

"Me and about every boy my age who went rushing home every afternoon to watch the Mickey Mouse Club. I was always disappointed when she wasn't featured. She was the first love of my life."

"Well, I am her distant cousin. I think my mother's cousin married a Funicello, or so I was told. Are you impressed?"

"Very. And you actually met her?"

"Yes. You may touch my arm if you wish."

He laughed. "You are amazing, Michaela Magliano Trueblood. Actress, pilot, Cherokee Princess and smart-ass all rolled up into one."

CHAPTER ELEVEN

Sheriff Abercorn said there was no real evidence to support any theory that Gus Creel was involved in the kidnapping, but he put the word out anyway. Sheriff's departments and county police were notified in the several Georgia counties surrounding Kalanu and in Tennessee and North Carolina where Creel had known relatives. There was no word of him. The consensus was that he hadn't been seen or heard from since he fled from the scene at the Creel Café, leaving behind a battered wife, a bloody shovel, and one unconscious police investigator.

"The family is lying," Tobias said. "They protect their own. He's been around."

"That may be so," Abercorn said. "But as yet we can't prove it. Just because he knows Jessop doesn't mean Gus Creel is part of this. I still have my reservations."

"I'm going to go have a talk with the ex-con that's on the list. He's working in Gainesville. Maybe you could have Owen look up a few of the other names. At least have him make some phone calls."

"I can do that. For someone who's on medical leave, you sure are busy. But go. Go with my blessing. Just stay out of that female reporter's way. I don't know why she's so mad at you, but she is."

"Don't blame me," Tobias said. "It's really Micki she's mad at."

"Just avoid her if possible," Abercorn said. "I have enough issues right now."

On the way out the door Micki put her hand on Tobias's elbow.

"Abby called the station."

"Yes."

"She's not my favorite person, but you should talk to her."

"It would get confusing right now," he said.

He knew she did not understand his reluctance, but a few minutes on the phone with Abby and she would wear him down. He would start to feel guilty. He would not be able to concentrate.

81

He knew instinctively he was missing something and he needed to keep focused until it became clear. Sharon Bishop's life might depend on it.

At the car he had less trouble with the seatbelts. Micki eased the car out onto the road and turned right. In the distance he heard a siren.

"My dad told me once you were the best police officer he'd ever know," Micki said. "He said you were good at what you did because you truly cared about finding the answers. He said you considered your job a calling. He also said it ruined all of your marriages."

"There haven't been that many marriages," he protested.

"So maybe you should call Abby," Micki said.

"Not yet," he said. "Tell me about this guy we're going to see. You read it. I only skimmed it. It still kind of hurts to read."

"He sounds like he's just a big, dumb kid who got into trouble because he dropped out of high school to get married and there was never enough money for his wife. So he started stealing things on the side to keep his wife in the luxuries she craved. For a while they lived the high life. Then he got caught and he went to prison. She divorced him, and now he drives an old car and works in a convenience store, and answers to his probation officer once or twice a month."

"Sounds like his divorce might be the one positive out of all of that," Tobias said.

The Four Corners Convenience Market was near the Holiday Inn in one of the less than attractive areas of Gainesville. The gas pumps were empty. There was only a rust covered Volkswagen parked out front. Across the street there was a brick house with the windows boarded up with plywood and knee-high grass in the front yard.

James Marx was alone in the store. He was big with a ruddy complexion and bad teeth. His brown hair was thinning on top. His eyes went over Tobias and dismissed him, but he couldn't seem to take his eyes off Micki.

"You're James Marx," Tobias said.

His eyes reluctantly went back to Tobias. "Who wants to know?"

82

Like James Cagney plays a gangster, Tobias thought. A big kid playing tough, but without anything substantial to back it up.

"I'm with the Kalanu County Sheriff's department," Tobias said. "We'd like to talk to you about what you told us on the phone earlier."

"Are you with the Sheriff's department, too?" Marx asked Micki.

"Yes," Micki said.

"It almost makes me want to be arrested again if you could put the handcuffs on," Marx said.

Micki only rolled her eyes. Tobias was proud of her self-control. He half expected her to shoot him.

"Try to concentrate, James," Tobias said. "You said you knew Clyde Jessop in jail?"

"I knew him, yeah," James said. "I didn't like him much. Nobody did. Nobody likes little creeps who mess with little girls." He licked his fat lips. "I like big girls myself."

Again, Micki only rolled her eyes.

"This is important, James," Tobias said. "And I'm tired. I don't want to drag your sorry butt to jail and lock you in a cell. I need this information and I need it now. So concentrate. You saw Jessop in jail. Tell me about it."

"What's there to tell?" he said. "I told everything on the phone. I saw Jessop a few times. He was in the same time I was. He didn't get around much. There were some guys who talked about beating him up, but he was being protected."

"By Gus Creel," Tobias said.

James Marx nodded. "Yeah. Gus Creel was there for a while. He got out a long time before us. But he was Jessop's cellmate for a while and nobody was going to mess with him. He was a monster. I saw him pick up a guy one time and pitch him over a table in the common room just like somebody else would swat a gnat. And with just one arm."

"And you say he protected Jessop?"

"Yeah. You know, sometimes it's like that with two guys who share a cell. One is like, you know, the woman, and her man protects her."

83

"It was like that with them," Tobias said, a little surprised. He had never thought Gus Creel was the type.

James Marx pursed his lips as if he was thinking deeply. It looked as if it pained him.

"I don't think so. It was something different. I don't know what it was but I don't think Creel had those kinds of feelings. But everybody knew not to mess with Jessop."

"But what about after Creel was released," Tobias said. "He couldn't protect him then."

Marx shrugged. "The prison grapevine. Word came that Jessop was to be left alone. Maybe money or drugs changed hand. I never knew the details, but he was left alone."

'What about Creel?" Tobias asked. "Was he into drugs?"

"I don't know. I don't think so. Probably a good thing, too."

"Why?"

"Creel was kind of crazy without the drugs. They talked about locking him up in the crazy ward once but I guess the guards figured he was okay as long as he didn't hurt anybody. I think the guards were kind of nervous around him."

"What did he do that was crazy?"

"He just acted crazy sometimes. You know he would sit on the ground during outside time and he would just stare up at the sky. Sometimes he said stuff that nobody could understand, you know like curses or something. We thought he was cursing the guards. And then once he took all his clothes off and he danced. That time the guards had to lock him up in the ward, but he didn't fight them. He went along with them, but he kept talking to himself."

"What else did he do?"

"Most of the time he was harmless," Marx said. "Most of his free time he read. But it was weird. He kept reading the same book over and over. He kept checking it out of the library so much that they finally just let him keep it all the time."

"What book was it?" Tobias said.

"I don't know. I never tried to find out. I think he took it with him when he left. Nobody wanted to try and get it back."

"Is there anything else you remember about him? Anything at all."

Marx shook his head. His eyes drifted back to Micki.

"Say," he said. "Are you some kind of Indian or something?'

"I'm a Mohican," Micki said.

James Marx looked puzzled. "I didn't think there were any of those left."

"I'm the very last one," Micki said sweetly.

CHAPTER TWELVE

"You still don't want me to call Abby?"

Tobias stubbornly shook his head. The last thing he wanted was for his wife to have any idea he was on the way to Creel's Café. It would probably send Abby into hysterics. The last time he had been at Creel's Café, he had lost more than a year of his life, and he feared it had changed something between him and Abby that he would never get back.

"You want to get a hamburger or something?" Micki asked. "I hear the food's good at the café."

"The cook would poison us," Tobias said.

"How about Hendricks' then?"

He nodded. He had not been thinking of food but it had been a long time since breakfast. Hendricks' was a few miles outside Gainesville, a one-time small, ranch-style home converted into a barbeque restaurant. There was no sign out front, only a bad image of a pig in the smoky window in front and Hendricks's written in bright red. It was one of those places people somehow find even without a lot of advertisement. The food was plentiful and tasty and cheap. There were very few tables for sitting, and no servers. Food was ordered at the counter and picked up there. When you were finished, you cleaned off your own table.

They both ordered cheeseburgers and fries and sat at a table in the rear to eat.

"You sure you want to go to the café?" Micki asked, between bites.

He shook his head. "I'm sure I don't. But I'm sure Creel's been back there. He wouldn't go long without visiting his mother. The Creels are big on family. Besides, that business about Kalanu taking the little girl to the Cloud Place. I've never heard of a Cloud Place. Maybe it's a family thing, and maybe his Momma will tell me."

"You don't really believe they'd tell you anything?" Micki said.

"I don't know. It's hard to tell what they will do. Even the family realizes Gus is crazy, and kidnapping little children is not like burglary or assault or selling moonshine. "

"Or hitting people in the head with shovels," Micki said.

"Yes," he said.

"I hate to admit Silverman's right about anything," Micki said, "but finding Gus might not save Sharon's life. She may already be dead at the bottom of a ravine somewhere."

"It's possible," he said.

"And both Sheriff Abercorn and your wife are going to be very unhappy with you when they find out we went to Creel's Café."

"I just know we're running out of time and the Cloud Place has something to do with all of this. After this, you can take me home and I'll make amends with Abby. I know she won't understand any of this, but I have to do this."

"Why?" Micki said.

Tobias gathered up the trash and stuffed it into a trash can near the door. The two of them walked back out to the Hummer. It was not until they were back on the highway that Micki repeated her question.

"Why do you have to do this? You were a good investigator. Maybe you were the best. But there are others who can do a competent job. Right now there are a lot of police officers hunting for Gus Creel. I'm sure they've already been out to the café and questioned the family a dozen times. What makes you think that you're going to find the answer when others can't?"

"I have to try," Tobias said.

"Give me a better reason other than you think you're some kind of super cop," Micki said.

"Because it's in my head somewhere," Tobias said. "I know it is. It's somewhere in the stories my grandfather told me. I grew up on these mountains. I hiked all over Kalanu Mountain before I was twelve years old."

"But you have a lot of trouble remembering all that stuff," Micki said. "Because a woman hit you in the head with the sharp edge of a shovel and you stayed in a coma for more than a year. When you woke up, you couldn't remember your name. You walked around in a fog for a couple of months. Right now you sometimes have trouble putting coherent thoughts together. And then there's Abby."

"What about Abby?'

Micki started to say something, but then she hesitated. His investigative skills were blunted, but it didn't take an investigator to know something had popped into her mind and then she thought better of saying it.

"What?" Tobias,

"Oh, nothing," Micki said. "It's none of my business. Let's go see the Creels. This should be interesting."

"It could be good for some laughs," Tobias said.

.....

Creel's Café was an ugly, squat three-story stone building at the edge of the highway. The building had been originally built as a grist mill by the first Augustus Creel, but it had never really operated profitably. It was said the real profit was in the moonshine stills up in the hills behind the grist mill. When Augustus died, it became little more than storage shed for years, but then another Creel had opened up a feed store which also was short-lived. For a time it had remained empty but then one of the granddaughters had inherited the property, and she had her husband had opened it as a café. The place had been completely remodeled. The bottom floor was gutted and hardwood floors were put down and a huge kitchen built. The upstairs were turned into living quarters.

The oldest of the three Creel brothers, Hugh, operated the café. It was rumored he still operated stills back in the hills that had once belonged to old Augustus, and that he sold the illegal whiskey under the counter. Hugh had never been caught doing anything illegal although both his brothers had a long history of burglary and theft and assault and pure drunken meanness.

A lot of people claimed the food served in the café was the best country style cooking they had ever eaten and tourists packed the place for three meals a day. Tobias had eaten there often as a kid with his grandfather, but not as an adult. He had arrested too many of the Creels to ever feel at ease in the place.

88

The café parking lot was gravel and sand. In the winter it washed away and left gaping potholes that made parking dangerous. Even out of season the café was popular, especially with the college students. Several college-aged kids were leaving as Micki parked. They were laughing and shouting as they piled into a Ford truck. There was barely room for them all, the girls half sitting in the boys laps. A couple of the girls glanced nervously at Mick as they left, as if half expecting her to flip on the blue lights and arrest them all.

"I doubt they're all wearing seatbelts," Micki said.

"You want to go arrest them?" Tobias asked.

"I'm not sure," Micki said, "would that make me a real deputy?"

"Yeah. Enough arrests like that, and you could run for Sheriff."

"A thankless job," Micki said, "I'd rather just fly my choppers."

"We probably should arrest every teenager who goes into Creel's," Tobias said bitterly. "I actually tried once to have the place put off limits by the college, but it came to nothing. I'm fairly sure Hugh sells whiskey to the kids, and I don't want to even think about upstairs."

"Upstairs?" Micki said.

"The Creels almost always have a couple of nieces staying with them. I expect the nieces are really working girls and the café makes a percentage of the profit."

"How does it stay open?" Micki asked.

"Because there is a Creel on the county commission and because money talks. The café caters a lot of business and political parties, almost for free. But it's a bit like making a bargain with the devil. Sooner or later the price has to be paid. I just hope it's not one of these kids."

There were only a few other cars in the parking lot as Tobias climbed out of the jeep. One was a bright red pick-up truck with jagged streaks of lighting painted on the side. Three young men stood near the truck and one of them turned to look toward Tobias. The young man was in his early twenties, hard and muscular, in tight jeans and a tight fitting T-shirt that showed off

89

his muscles. He had blond hair and bright blue eyes. The other two young men standing nearby were copycats, younger, less muscular, and less aggressive in their postures.

"Alpha male," Micki said.

"His name is George Washington Creel. He's Hugh's oldest kid. He's Gus Creel's nephew. His friends call him Bubba."

"You've got to be kidding," Micki said. "He drives a red pickup truck and his name is Bubba. I hope he doesn't play a banjo because I think I saw this in Deliverance."

"Don't make the mistake of thinking he's a clown," Tobias said.

"Oh, I won't," Micki said. "You know, he's very good looking. He's a movie star type."

"Bubba doesn't resemble his dad, or either of his uncles. In fact, he doesn't look like a Creel. No trace of the old Cherokee blood."

"Perhaps a different generic pool?" Micki suggested.

"Yeah. I think an entirely different generic pool."

"Are you suggesting his mother might not have been entirely faithful to her husband?"

"Just making conversation," Tobias said.

The three young men moved to block their way. Bubba had his muscular arms folded across his chest. He was grinning. His two friends tried to adopt the same posture, but both of them looked nervous.

"The cops have already been here asking about Gus," Bubba said. "We haven't seen him. So why don't you get back in your car and leave."

"Move out of the way, Bubba," Tobias said. "I've got no time for you today."

"You're not welcome here," he said. "You should have learned the last time. Now why don't you and the Indian bitch get back in the car before you get hurt?"

Tobias started to respond that he was there on official business, but he had no opportunity to say the words. He caught a flash out of the corner of his eye and was again surprised at Micki's quickness. It wasn't speed, so much. She might not have been able to outrun a popped up baseball to first base, but it was

90

the kind of quickness that enabled an elite NFL running back to pick the right opening in a defensive line and burst through it before it closed again. It was sudden, unexpected and savage.

Barely seconds later, Bubba was hopping around and squealing like an injured pig from where Micki had stamped down on his instep. Her second kick was between his legs and Tobias flinched as he saw the power behind it. Bubba squealed again and went down to his knees. His face was a peculiar greenish color and then Micki jumped back as he began vomiting up his lunch

Micki turned to the other two young men but they were backing away quickly. They wanted nothing to do with her, and Tobias couldn't blame them. The soft sweetness of her Italian heritage had disappeared, and only the Cherokee showed in her features. Her eyes seemed almost black with fury, her lips drawn back in a savage grimace that was truly frightening. Even Tobias had to fight an impulse to back away from her. It was a little like being in a cage with a snarling wolf.

Micki ignored the two young men and took Bubba by his long hair. He had stopped vomiting, but his eyes were sick and dull with pain.

"I am a duly appointed semi-official deputy with the Kalanu County police department," Micki said softly. "I am not an Indian bitch, and if you ever again refer to me that way or tell me that I'm not welcome anywhere, I will take it personally and I will cut them off and feed them to you in small bites. Blink your eyes if you understand."

He blinked his eyes. She released him and rubbed her hand across the rump of her jeans. It still took a moment for her face to relax to normal.

"You are a little scary," Tobias said.

She smiled. The smile definitely changed her face.

"Nah."

"Was all that really necessary?" he asked. "I think eventually he would have listened to reason."

"He's a big fellow," Micki said. "My husband was a big fellow. He never listened to reason. I found out I could avoid pain by hitting him first and hardest. It seems to work better for me that

91

way. It's not like in the movies. I can't dance around and do high karate kicks and take on seven guys at a time. I have to hit first."

"Aniwaya," Tobias said.

"What does that mean?"

"It's Cherokee. It means you're of the wolf clan."

Micki repeated the words. "Of the wolf clan. I kind of like that."

"I thought you might," he said. "My grandfather told stories about the most savage warriors being of the wolf clan. They were sort of like Viking Berserkers. Kalanu was supposedly of the wolf clan."

"But then your grandfather was sometimes full of it," Micki said.

"Exactly," Tobias said.

Inside the café was pleasantly warm and surprisingly clean. The hardwood floors were polished. White tablecloths covered the tables. A couple of young, attractive waitresses served the tables and from the kitchen there were good smells.

"I've never been in here before," Micki said. "It's kind of nice."

"Yeah," Tobias said, "Miss April runs a taunt ship."

The walls were also wood but covered with a lot of old metal advertising slogans and posters and photos from past years. There were old Coca-Cola signs with polar bears and pretty girls. There were only a few customers enjoying a late lunch. Near the front door was a cash register with a large display of T-shirts, coffee cups, and baseball caps all with Creel Café imprinted on them. Behind the register Hugh Creel watched them. Short and squat, sixtyish, he had thick, broad shoulders and a thick neck. He had once wrestled professionally under the name, Axe Man, but for the past twelve years he had managed the day-to-day operations of the café. His eighty year old mother still held ownership, but she seldom came in except for meals.

At a nearby table another short, muscular looking man got to his feet. Andrew Jackson Creel was Hugh's oldest son, a mean-tempered drunk who had been arrested several times for different crimes. He was suspected in burglaries as far away as Fulton County, but had never been convicted. Tobias knew he helped in his father's moonshine business, and was probably the pimp for the girls brought in from Atlanta, but again nothing had ever been proved.

Tobias thought it was only a matter of time. Andrew was too stupid not to get caught sooner or later.

Sitting across from Andrew was his wife Kate. Kate was small, pale, dispirited. Tobias had known and liked Kate as a young woman who had occasionally worked as a waitress in the Mountain Laurel Café. She made good grades at school but she was from a dirt-poor back woods family where the girls got married too young and had babies and the babies got married too young. It was a never ending cycle of ignorance and poverty, and Kate was a victim.

She had never been beautiful but she had appealing with a fresh innocence. She had dreamed of leaving Kalanu and getting an education. She wanted to find a job in Atlanta. Instead she had met Andrew Creel and was pregnant soon after. Only a vague shadow remained of the Kate he remembered. Life had soured her.

There were two other men sitting at the table with Hugh, both of them squat and overweight, but with powerful forearms and shoulders. Tobias suspected their upper body strength was due to years of lifting hundred pound bags of corn mash and carrying them up narrow trails to where the stills were built.

"You want something, Atkins?"

"Sit down, son," Hugh Creel said, and Andrew settled back into his chair. He put his large, rough hand on his wife's knee as if to point out his possession to Tobias. Kate took no notice of him. Her eyes were looking dull and empty. She seemed to be looking off in the distance at something only she was seeing.

"I would recommend the meat loaf today," Hugh said. "It's delicious. Our very own recipe. And you won't find better sweet corn anywhere. The stewed tomatoes are a little off. We buy them fresh, but I haven't been getting the best product lately. I may have to change my supplier."

"I had a late lunch," Tobias said.

"Then this must be a social call," Hugh said. "And here all this time I've been thinking you didn't like us."

"I like you just fine, Hugh," Tobias said. "You are a great bunch of folks."

"No bad memories of the last time you were here," Hugh scrunched up his face as if he was trying to remember something. "Oh, wait. I hear you don't have memories at all."

Everyone at the table, except Kate, laughed.

"I remember enough," Tobias said.

Hugh shook his head. "I don't feel bad for you, Swede. You had no business being here. It was a family matter. We would have settled it ourselves. Now I've got a sister-in-law in jail because of you."

"She shouldn't have been having sexual relations with her nephew."

'That's a damned lie," Hugh said.

"Gus believed it was true. That was why he was knocking her around in the parking lot. It's why he ran away afterwards. But I'm pretty sure he didn't stay away. I expect he's been around."

Hugh shook his head. "I haven't seen him."

"I don't think you're being completely honest, Hugh."

"You want honesty. I'll be honest. I wish Lilly had hit you a lot harder with that shovel."

"I'm sure you do, but it was really my fault. I violated the first rule of police work."

"What's that?"

"Never, ever turn your back on a Creel."

Hugh's face grew ugly. "What the hell do you want here this time?"

"I want Gus."

"I told you. He hasn't been around."

"He's your brother, Hugh. I understand he is family and you want to protect him. But this time he's involved in something nasty. There's a little girl missing."

"My brother wouldn't have bothered that little girl," Hugh insisted.

"Your family has been outspoken against the Windfall Project. I believe you even made a statement about it. Didn't you call it destroying your heritage or something like that?"

"What's that got to do with anything?"

"You're not thinking clearly, Hugh. A lot of officials might look the other way at a few of your activities, but not kidnapping children. The newspapers find out that Gus was really involved in this and all the politicians who support you are going to start running for cover. Nobody's going to want to be associated with you."

For the first time Tobias saw a look of doubt in Hugh's eyes. Hugh had gone on to the seventh grade in school before he quit, but he had a different kind of education. He had an instinctive awareness of any kind of threat to the family, and he was sly enough to avoid it most of the time. This was something different and it was clear he had not considered all the consequences until that moment.

"So somebody made a phone call for Gus," Tobias said.

In poker it would have been called a give because Hugh's nervous eyes went involuntarily to his son and then he jerked his head back around to face Tobias.

'Sharon Bishop's father is serving in combat overseas," Tobias said.

"So?"

"He's a hero, Hugh. You think how that is going to look if that girl dies and Gus is found responsible."

"My brother didn't do this," Hugh said.

"Where is he?" Tobias asked.

"I don't know. I tell you, he didn't do this."

"Where is the Cloud Place?"

Hugh looked genuinely puzzled. "I've never heard of that. What is it?'

The front door opened and Bubba came hobbling in. He was pale and still in obvious pain. For the first time Kate showed animation in her face. She was up out her chair in a moment and putting her arm around him to give him support. Tobias felt sick inside as he watched her suddenly expressive features, her dark eyes looking up at her nephew with something more than an aunt and a nephew. It was happening again, Tobias realized, and this time the husband wasn't in prison.

Tobias glanced at Andrew. Bubba's older brother looked flushed, and there was a tightening around the eyes. His hands were gripping the edge of the table. Any second Tobias thought Andrew was going to come across the table after his brother, but somehow Andrew controlled his temper. There was definitely more trouble brewing. Bubba seemed to have a strong attraction to his sister in laws.

Tobias felt suddenly weak and tired and sour. His head was still hurting. It seemed he had spent a lifetime arresting somebody in the Creel family or trying to stop them from hurting themselves or others. He had lived and worked in Savannah, Georgia, for a time when he was younger, and the Creels were like those annoying black gnats that swarmed on humid summer evenings. They kept coming back no matter how many times they were brushed away.

"What happened to you?" Hugh asked.

Bubba's eyes went accusingly to Micki, but then he actually blushed. He stayed silent. Micki looked amused. It was obvious that admitting Micki put him down so easily in the parking lot would have made him a creature of derision rather than sympathy. These kinds of men did not admire weakness. His status as an alpha male would be forever challenged.

"I fell down," he said.

Kate put her arm tighter around his waist and she led him off through the café and into the back where there were stairs leading up to the living quarters. Andrew Creel watched them go, his eyes hurt and angry.

Tobias sighed. There would be trouble but this time it would not be him who answered the call when Andrew Creel and his brother starting fighting. He only hoped the deputy kept an eye on Kate in the process. Kate was a meek little lamb but even meek little lambs sometimes turned into raging lions when family was concerned.

"I want to talk to Miss April," Tobias said.

"Nobody's stopping you," Hugh said. "But she doesn't know where Gus is either. And she doesn't have any more use for you than I do."

"She's at home?"

"She's at home," Hugh said. "Just watch for shovels."

"You're a funny man, Hugh."

"I have a great sense of humor," Hugh said. "Hell, I'm even funnier than you know. In fact, I want to show you something you'll appreciate. I thought of it myself."

From under the counter Hugh brought out a black jewelry case. Opening it, he placed it on the counter so Tobias and Micki could see inside. A silver charm rested on a background of red velvet. It was in the shape of a miniature shovel. Andrew Creel laughed out loud.

"I'm selling them at five dollars a pop and I've already sold out the first order I had made," he said. "I'm doubling my order this time. You know, you're a very popular guy in the counter. Even the Mount Rawls mayor brought one for his wife. She said it was pretty."

"I do like your entrepreneurial spirit, Hugh."

"Of course it's a little like one of those paintings that sell better if the artists is dead. I would have made a fortune if you hadn't survived the coma."

"Sorry to disappoint you, Hugh."

"No matter," Hugh said. "It's not like you're looking all that healthy. There's still a chance."

"Optimism is always good."

CHAPTER THIRTEEN

Behind the café Tobias and Micki followed a narrow grassy path through thick strands of pine trees. The path was a quarter mile long and there were a dozen no-trespassing signs nailed to trees along the way. Each of the signs had a skull and crossbones insignia and a few had hands with pistols pointing toward the trail with the words, "this means you."

"They're not a friendly bunch," Micki said.

"Even less than you realize," Tobias said. "Somewhere nearby is a guy watching us with a shotgun."

"Seriously," Micki said "this is becoming more and more like the movies."

"Why did you think I stopped long enough to tell Hugh I was coming out to see his mother? I didn't want anybody to mistake my little visit for a raid. Hugh has his moonshine stills somewhere around here, and it's not a safe thing to be wandering around. "

"He's vermin," Micki said savagely.

"Careful what you say. The Creels are part Cherokee, you know. Of course everybody in Georgia claims to be related to a Cherokee princess somewhere in their background, but the Creels settled here even before the removal and they took Cherokee wives and husbands. So they may be distantly related to you."

"Thanks for pointing that out. That makes me feel warm all over." She touched his shoulder to make him halt for a moment. "There's a great deal I still don't understand. They didn't teach Cherokee history at the convent school. I heard you mention the removal. I heard the same word from someone else not long ago, and it was mentioned in your grandfather's story. What was the removal?"

"Okay. Short history lesson. For the in-depth study, you might want to attend a few of Hattie's courses. But the crux of it was the Cherokee got here first although some believe there were even older tribes before them. That's another history lesson. But the Cherokee were not like other Native Americans who resisted the white man. The Cherokee were smart. They adapted. They became one of the Five Civilized Tribes. They owned land and businesses and lived in nice homes. They had their own newspaper and their own written alphabet."

"Sequoyah," Micki said. "I have heard of him."

"Yes. He created the alphabet. But to make a long story short, the newly arrived white settlers wanted the land the Cherokees already had and the Government decided to move the entire nation of Cherokees and the other civilized tribes to reservations in Oklahoma. The Army came and gathered them up and forced marched them all the way to Oklahoma. The Cherokee call it the Trail of Tears."

"That's horrific," Micki said.

"Yes. But my grandfather used to say that out of the most terrible circumstances come the stories of the greatest courage and commitment. Out of the greatest tribulation, comes our greatest strength. Take Sequoyah, for example. He was a poor half-breed cripple named George Gist. His mother was Cherokee but his father was an English fur-trader. He was given the name Sequoyah because it means pig's foot in Cherokee. Because of his handicap from a hunting accident, he ended up becoming a craftsman and though he could never read or write English, he developed the Cherokee alphabet. Out of tribulation comes the strength."

"You really love this place, don't you?" Micki asked. "You really love the stories, and the history."

"I guess it was one of the gifts my grandfather gave to me," he said.

"And my father? Did he also grow up with those stories?"

"Yes," Tobias said abruptly.

The sudden harshness of his tone did not invite anymore questions.

Miss April's house was a small, red-brick, ranch-style at the end of the path. She lived alone and took her meals in the café. Nearly ninety, tiny, silver-haired, she made the walk to the café three times a day with the help of a cane. She came out on her small front porch to meet them as they approached, and did not look happy to see them.

"What do you want?"

"I need to ask you about Gus," Tobias said.

"I told those other policeman already. I haven't seen Gus. My son doesn't come around here anymore, and it's your fault. "

"There's a little girl lost on the mountain. Some think she's already dead. I think Gus took her."

Miss April shook her head. "Gus wouldn't harm a child."

"Maybe not in his right mind," Tobias said. "But right now he's not in his right mind. Right now he thinks he's some kind of witch"

"What nonsense are you talking?"

"He thinks he's the spirit of the mountain. He thinks he's Kalanu. He's trying to stop the Windfall project by kidnapping a child in the same way the original Kalanu was supposed to have driven the early settlers from the mountain."

Miss April shook her head sadly. "Maybe you'd better come in. I can't stand for a long time."

Tobias had never been invited into the house before. The inside was neat and clean. She led them into the kitchen where she told them to sit, and she poured them all coffee. Tobias was aware of a subtle change in her he didn't trust. Miss April might seem like a harmless elderly woman, but she still had a sharp mind and an animal cunning. Her husband had been a skinny, mean-tempered man who had twice been sent to prison for burglary. Tobias often wondered if there was some weird genetic fault in this part of the Creel family that led them all toward crime and madness.

The coffee was good.

"I had four sons," she said. "James was my oldest but he died in Korea. They gave him the Silver Star. Luke was next but he was mean like his daddy and he's serving time in Texas. Hugh's the baby, and then there's Gus. Gus was a big baby, and he just kept getting bigger. Maybe he just grew too fast for his mind but he was always a little slower than the others. He had a lot of trouble in school, but he had a strong back and he could do the work of three men."

"Where would he go on the mountain?" Tobias asked.

"He loves that mountain like your grandfather loved it," she said. "He could be anywhere."

"And you're telling the truth. He hasn't been back here, not even to use the phone."

"Who would he call?" she asked.

"He might call the newspapers or he might have called the mother of the little girl he kidnapped."

"I can't believe Gus would do that. It's not in his nature."

"The girl's name is Sharon Bishop. Her father is currently serving in the military overseas. I imagine they've contacted him by now, and maybe flying him back home. When he stands in front of the press, there's going to be hell to pay. This time there are going to be no friendly politicians to help you. This is not illegal alcohol or prostitutes from Atlanta."

"I don't know what you're talking about," she said.

There had been a momentary flicker in her eyes when he mentioned the name Sharon Bishop.

He had questioned enough people to know she had somehow recognized the name.

"What do you know of the little girl?" Tobias asked quickly.

"What could I possibly know?"

"You've heard her name. Sharon Bishop."

"No."

Tobias knew she wasn't going to answer, and he suspected all her protective instincts were on alert. She might have been concerned for Gus, but she was already considering how the family would be affected by this. If Gus had kidnapped the child, it was the worst kind of crime imaginable, and this time people would not look the other way. But she wasn't going to answer how she knew about Sharon Bishop. Tobias had a feeling he already knew the answer.

"Gus has come back here, hasn't he?" Tobias said. "He comes back for food sometimes."

"He's been back," Miss April admitted. "He's my child. I wouldn't let him go hungry."

"But you don't know where he is on the mountain?"

She shook her head.

"There must be someplace he likes going."

"He knows the mountain," she said. "He's gone off by himself up there ever since he was little. He could be anywhere."

"Have you ever heard him speak of a Cloud Place?" Tobias asked.

"A Cloud Place. No. I've never heard of anything like that. There used to be a shop over in Mount Rawls called Cloud Place or Cloud Park, something like that."

"It's someplace on the mountain," Tobias said.

"I've never heard of it," she insisted.

"And you've never heard of Sharon Bishop."

"No."

She was very tough and he knew he had learned all he could from her. Perhaps she knew where Gus was, but she wasn't going to admit it.

"If you hear from Gus, you'll call the department," Tobias said.

"Of course," she said.

He didn't believe it for a moment. She walked them to the door. She didn't say goodbye. On the porch she shut the door behind them, lock clicking into place.

"She's an odd woman," Micki said.

"You don't know the half of it." Tobias said.

"Did you notice her wrist?"

"What about her wrist?" Tobias asked.

"She had a charm bracelet. It had about a dozen of those little shovels dangling from it."

CHAPTER FOURTEEN

In the car Micki could not get hold of Sheriff Abercorn. She talked to a deputy for a few minutes and then rang off.

"It seems Harvey took a nap and a shower and he's back up on the mountain. Silverman has his entire unit up there now, and he seems to be running things. There's still a lookout for Gus Creel but he hasn't been spotted. "

Tobias nodded. His head hurt, and was getting worse. He knew he was reaching the end of his endurance. It had been a long time since he had moved around so much. He also kept trying hard to remember anything he had ever heard about a Cloud Place. He knew there was something but it remained elusive and the harder he tried to remember, the harder his head hurt.

"Are you okay?" Micki asked.

"Yeah," he lied. "She knew Sharon Bishop."

"Who?"

"Miss April. She knew Sharon, or she'd heard the name."

"So what does that mean to us?"

"It means that Gus either told her recently or she knew the name before. I don't think Gus told her. I think it was a surprise to her or she would have done a better job of covering up. So there's somehow a connection between Gus and Sharon Bishop."

"How did Sharon Bishop get chosen out of all the girls in the valley," Micki said.

"Exactly," Tobias said.

"He knew her. Gus knew her somehow."

"Or the mother," Tobias said.

Micki was silent for a moment. Tobias knew they were both thinking the same thing and neither of them wanted to say it out loud. Micki started the car and turned west along the highway. Tobias didn't have to ask where they were going.

"The timing is hard to figure out," Tobias said. "Gus was released from prison in late September. He came home to find out his wife had been getting really cozy with his nephew. He gets mad and starts punching his wife around in the parking lot."

"Why didn't he punch the nephew," Micki interrupted.

"What?"

"The nephew was just as much to blame. Why didn't he punch the nephew?"

"I hadn't really thought about it much," Tobias admitted.

"Male chauvinist thing. The wife was the one to blame. She should have controlled her baser instincts. The nephew was only doing what came natural."

"Probably something like that," Tobias said. "And then I show up on my white charger. Lilly clobbers me, gets sent to prison, and Gus runs for the hills. So when and how would he have seen Sharon.

"Before he went to prison?" Micki suggested.

"No. The timing is still not right. Something in the pattern doesn't fit."

"No?"

"If we are right and it is Gus who has Sharon."

"I think we are, "Micki said. "I think we're going to have to talk to the Mom."

. "Yeah."

"But Harvey won't like it."

"No. He'll have a fit."

"But we're going to do it anyway."

"There's an old saying that if you want to get something done, it's always better to ask forgiveness than permission."

"Works for me," Micki said.

.....

It was getting colder and even the blankets were not enough. Through the open door of the shelter she could see occasional snow flurries. Earlier a deer had stepped into the clearing and stood looking at her for a few moments before turning and bounding back into the thick growth. There was no other sign of life, and no sound. It was incredible how silent everything was.

She had tried yelling to break the silence but nobody came, no matter how loud she yelled. She finally stopped because the yelling dissolved into tears and now her throat felt raspy.

She was scared. Her heart beat fast and she had to take deep breaths to calm herself down. She was also getting terribly hungry and she still had to go to the bathroom.

"Somebody, please help me," she yelled again, but her voice came out as an ineffective whisper.

．．．．．

Karen Bishop was a lot younger than Tobias had imagined her. She might have been pretty with a little make-up, her hair combed, and a nice dress, but sitting across from him on the couch, she looked washed-out. She wore a shapeless grey dress and she was barefoot. Her legs were curled underneath her on the couch in a position only the very young or the very limber could manage. Her reddened eyes were puffy.

"Have you found out anything about Sharon?" Karen asked.

"No, I'm sorry, Mrs. Bishop," Tobias said. "We're still searching on the mountain."

"It's going to be cold up there again tonight," Karen said.

"We're doing everything we can,' Tobias said. "I just have a couple of questions. First, are you sure you didn't recognize the voice on the phone?"

She shook her head. "No, I'm sure I never heard the voice before."

"Okay. Then do you know a man named Gus Creel."

She shook her head. "I don't think so. Is he related to Miss April?"

"You know Miss April," Tobias asked.

"I met her at the apple festival," Karen said. "She makes the greatest apple butter. She tried to teach me the recipe but it never turned out right for me. I guess I'm not the world's greatest chef."

"Gus Creel is her son," Tobias said.

"I could have met him," Karen said. "I just don't remember. You think he has something to do with Karen's kidnapping?"

"We're not sure," Tobias said. "His name just came up in the investigation."

"How long as your husband been deployed, Mrs. Bishop?" Micki asked abruptly.

Tobias glanced up irritably. The tone of her voice sounded harsh. Micki was standing at a nearby dresser looking at wedding photos. Tobias noticed one of them was of Karen, her new husband, and Sharon as a flower girl.

"Almost a year and a half," Karen Bishop said.

"Why couldn't he have come home when everybody else did?"

"He could have come home with the others, but he said it was important that he finish what he was working on. As if somebody else couldn't do it. Now, I don't know what the college will do."

"What about the college?" Tobias asked.

"Well, he had a good job teaching. That's how he met. I was one of his students. He was recently widowed and he just looked so distinguished and so lonely. Things just happened."

"How did you get along with Sharon?" Micki asked.

"She called me Karen, and that was okay. I wasn't trying to replace her mother. I thought we were becoming friends."

Friends, Tobias thought. Friends with a little girl who had recently lost her mother, and now had an interloper in the household. A little girl who was already conflicted and confused. And then her father gone, deployed in a far off fight she wouldn't have understood. So things at home could not have been entirely pleasant for either of them.

"Do you have any family nearby, Mrs. Bishop?"

"No," Karen Bishop said. "I was an only child. I lost my dad in a car accident when I was a baby and my mother passed away only a few years ago. All of my husband's people live in South Carolina."

"So I guess it's been pretty lonely."

"Yes," Karen said.

In his mind Tobias was yelling at Micki to stop, that couldn't she see her questions were only making things worse. Then the pattern started becoming clear and he realized she was asking the kind of question he should have been asking. Instinctively Micki saw what he should have seen.

"I don't imagine Sharon made things easier," Micki said.

"No," Karen admitted. "There were times when I think she blamed me for her father being away. It was hard for her to understand. It was hard for me to understand. We were only married a few months. We hadn't even had a honeymoon yet. We were planning to go at the end of the school term and then they called him up.'

"So how did you pass the time?" Micki said.

"I kept busy doing charity stuff, and I had a part time job at the college doing filing. I kept busy."

"No friends?" Micki said.

"Of course I had friends," Karen said.

"Any male friends?" Micki said bluntly.

Karen was instantly defensive. Her body tightened up. Her small hands rested on her knees and they clenched into fists. Her eyes went desperately from Micki to Tobias and back again. Tobias felt sorry for her as if he himself was adding to her already considerable burden.

"I don't know what you mean by that," Karen said.

"What she means is we have to know who you know, Karen," Tobias said softly. "It's possible that it was one of your friends involved in this, or even a casual acquaintance."

Her body did not relax. Tears flowed down her face and she buried her face in her hands with a convulsive sob. Micki went over and sat beside her on the couch, her intimidating manner gone. She pulled Karen into her arms and held her while she cried. Over her shoulder she met Tobias's eyes.

"It's going to be all right now, Karen," Micki said. "You just tell us what happened."

"It was only one time," Karen said. "I swear it was only time."

Her face was buried in Micki's shoulder, and her voice sounded far away.

"Who?" Micki said.

"Miss April sent him over with some apple butter for me, and he was just so handsome and funny, and I was so lonely. It was just one time, and now God is punishing me."

"You're talking about Bubba Creel," Tobias said.

"It was just one time," Karen wailed.

Karen jumped up from the couch and rushed to her bedroom. Micki followed. The bedroom was at the end of a narrow hallway and Tobias saw Karen throw herself down on the bed. Micki sat on the bed beside her. Tobias turned his back and looked out the window. There were kids playing in an empty lot across the street. He could hear Micki's voice, but he could not distinguish her words.

He turned from the window and examined all the pictures on the dresser. There was another picture there, a picture of a woman with dark hair and a wide smile. She was sitting in a rocking chair in front of looked like a Cracker Barrel Restaurant. She was holding a child. Sharon's mother perhaps, a constant reminder to Karen that she was not the true mother. Probably just one of the reminders she was given every day.

Karen returned with Micki. She had washed her face. She sat primly on the couch, knees crossed, but without the defensive posture. Submissive, now. Acceptance.

"I'll answer your questions," she said.

"Did you know Gus Creel," Tobias asked for the second time.

'No," she said. "Micki explained that Gus is Bubba's brother, but I didn't meet him. There was someone who stayed in the truck outside the day Bubba came, but I never met him. It could have been Gus."

"Could the man in the truck have seen Sharon?"

Karen looked miserable and nodded. "Sharon was outside playing the entire time. He could have seen her. He probably did. I guess this really is my fault."

"Why? Because you made a mistake? We all make mistakes."

"Yeah, sure," she said.

"Listen to me, Karen," Tobias said gently. "People make mistakes every day. We all show poor judgment. None of us are perfect. You didn't make the wrath of God come down on your head just because you slept with Bubba Creel."

"I bet my husband won't feel so forgiving when he comes home," Karen said bitterly.

There were a lot of other things he could have said but Karen was not listening. She was caught up in her sense of helplessness and guilt. And he expected she was right. Her husband was not going to feel that way when he returned home.

Outside, Tobias breathed deeply of the clear, clean air. It made his head feel a little better. Neither he nor Micki spoke much as they walked back to the car. Somewhere in the distance a crow cawed at them.

"I grew up Catholic," Micki said. "I never had many problems with that kind of guilt."

"I grew up going to a small little Baptist church back in the hills. My parents were there every time the door opened. I must have heard the sermon about how Jesus took the sins of the world onto the cross a thousand times."

"And you don't believe that," Micki said.

"The problem is human nature."

"How?"

"We keep trying to take them back."

CHAPTER FIFTEEN

Deputy Art Palmer was late getting to work. The harsh weather had caught him by surprise and he had been forced to detour around an already closed mountain road. When he walked into the sheriff's department, he knew immediately it was going to be a bad night. Sergeant Gail Mathis was still on duty and the watch commander was on the road working an accident. The department usually ran more officers on the middle shift because those were the busiest, but with many deputies involved in the mountain search, everyone was getting overtime.

Deputy Art Palmer did not much like Mathis. He didn't think women belonged in uniform, and he especially resented taking orders from a woman who had less time in grade than he had. He had complained loudly when the department had chosen Mathis for the strikes instead of several other officers who had more time and experience, but Abercorn had called him into the office for a brief conversation and he had stopped complaining … out loud.

He still resented her.

"Jessop's in the waiting room," she said, as soon as she saw him. "Take him back to the holding cell."

"What's he doing in the waiting room?" Palmer complained.

"His lawyer had to see him," Mathis explained. "I had another deputy watching him, but I had to put him on the road. It's a mess out there tonight."

"That little creep doesn't deserve a lawyer," Parker said.

"Probably not, but we're just the working class, Deputy Palmer. We don't get to play judge."

"Things would be better off if we could sometimes," Palmer said.

Her look showed her irritation with him. "Right now I don't have time for a lot of political issues. Just make sure you follow procedure. You remember the memo about procedure, don't you? People have been getting a little lax lately."

She stared at him, waiting for an answer.

"I remember," he said finally.

"You make sure Jessop is handcuffed when you take him down."

"All right," he said irritably.

"Then go. We're short-handed downstairs too. Only Jack is down there now."

There were supposed to be two deputies in the dungeon at all times. In the day watch there were more.

"Where's Tyler?" he asked.

"Called in sick."

Palmer shook his head. Another irritation he would have to put up with. Tyler was quiet and he seldom complained if asked to do extra. Palmer was able to nap and now and then with Tyler on duty but Jack Mathis was a different story. Jack Mathis was married to Gail Mathis, the desk sergeant. Nobody who worked in the department was supposed to be married but Jack and Gail had met on the job. They now had two children, and Jack was in line to make sergeant when the day watch sergeant retired or when Gail took on the position of watch commander. Life wasn't fair.

The phone rang and she answered it. Her attention was on the screen behind the desk where all of the dispatched calls for both fire and police were showing up. He watched her for a few moments. He might not have appreciated her as a police supervisor, but he appreciated the way she filled out a uniform. She was a petite honey-blonde who looked like she belonged on the stage of a beauty pageant thanking people for electing her the queen of the festival.

She felt his eyes on her and looked up and he figured it was time to move along.

He stopped at the door to interview room one and looked in the small window. Jessop was sitting quietly at a table. He thought he might have time for a quick cigarette before he had to take him down. Smoking was not allowed in the building and once he got downstairs, it would be four hours before he could come back up for lunch.

The back door was automatic. It released from the inside, but only by inserting a key card in the lock. The problem was that you could not use a key card to get back in. Just outside the door there was a brick used for the purpose of keeping the door open while the officers smoked. Palmer pushed it between the frame and the door and stepped outside.

He pulled his uniform jacket tighter around him as the cold seeped through. He lit the cigarette and smoked it slowly, watching the shadows play along the top of Mount Rawls.

He thought of the little girl somewhere up there on one of those cold mountain tops. He was glad it wasn't him.

He finished off the cigarette and squashed the butt against the wall. He sighed. It was time to move Jessop.

Inside, he unlocked the heavy door and stepped inside. Jessop looked up at him. Jessop looked as if he was in pain. In fact, he looked as if he had been crying.

"You all right," he asked.

Jessop did not respond.

"Who were you expecting? Kalanu?"

Palmer laughed at his own joke. Everybody had heard the story Jessop had told, and nobody believed it. Especially not Palmer. Palmer thought it was a bunch of nonsense. Ghost stories had never scared him, not even as a child. He would have been surprised if someone had told him that one of his failures was his lack of imagination. He could not imagine anything he could not see, hear or taste. His lack of imagination also prohibited him from seeing things that might happen.

Such as Jessop bolting like a scared rabbit.

"I don't have time to mess with you," Palmer said, and he put his hand on Jessop's shoulder and pulled it from the chair. He knew he should follow the procedure and handcuff the skinny little man. But it seemed foolish. Jessop could barely walk. Besides, he wasn't going to allow Mathis to tell him how to perform his duties. He had been a police officer long than she had.

He was not prepared when Jessop gave a violent twist and then rammed him hard in the chest.

He was already off balance. He went skidding to the floor and Jessop was gone, through the doorway in a moment. With a sinking sensation, he realized he had left the brick in the back door. He scrambled frantically to his feet and ran after Jessop but he was too late. Jessop was out the back door.

"The damned idiot," Palmer said.

There was still no place for Jessop to go. The little enclosure in the back was surrounded by a fence and there was no gate. Palmer rubbed his chest where Jessop had hit him, and he stepped outside.

There was no place to go. It was stupid,

But he saw that Clyde Jessop had done the impossible. With the agility of an NBA player, Clyde had jumped and caught the bottom rung of an old metal ladder that was used for workmen to gain access to the roof. The roof was flat asphalt and during rainy weather, it developed a lot of leaks. The bottom rung was at least eight feet off the ground and thought impossible for anybody to reach without an additional ladder, but somehow Jessop was pulling himself up.

"There's no place to go," Palmer said. "You'll just have to come back down."

Palmer found the situation almost funny. The skinny little guy was going to have to climb back down eventually because there was no other access to the roof. It was all a waste of effort and time.

Mathis had heard Palmer hollering and had come to the back to see what the problem was. She got there in time to see Jessop reach the top rung of the ladder and then scamper like a monkey over the edge of the roof. Her face grew pale.

"Go after him," she said.

"Why?" Palmer said. "He's got no way off the roof. He'll come down sooner or later."

"That's what I'm afraid of," Mathis said. "Look, there's a ladder in the storage room. Get it and go up after him. And the watch commander is going to want to know why he's not wearing cuffs and how the back door got open. I hope you've got some good answers."

Up until that moment Parker had not been greatly concerned. Now he could feel an overwhelming sense of rage toward Jessop. The little man was about to get him into serious

113

trouble. He was fifty-three, a little overweight, and out of shape. He had violated procedure by escorting Jessop to his cell without putting him in handcuffs.

Why did he have to run?

There was no place to go and he would have to come back down the same way.

Unless.

He started to understand what Mathis meant and a sense of panic surged through him. Hurriedly he went to the storeroom and found the ladder crammed in the back against a corner. It seemed to take him hours to get it out and he left boxes in the hall as he took it back outside again. He pressed it against the wall and went up and grabbed the bottom rung of the ladder.

Climbing up was harder than he thought. The metal rungs were like ice. Mathis came out into the yard and told him the watch supervisor was on the way and they were to get Jessop off the building if they could.

"He wanted to know how the hell he got up there," Mathis said.

Parker cringed. He knew that question would keep being asked, and if Jessop did something really stupid... it might mean his job.

Mathis climbed faster. At the top he had trouble getting over the edge of the room and he caught his uniform on a rusty roofing nail and ripped it down the side, along with his leg. He finally managed to scramble onto the flat roof and he stood up. Jessop was over on the far side of the roof, looking up at the mountains.

"Come on now," Parker said softly. "Come on now, buddy. Let's go back down now. It's cold up here. Let's go down where it's warm."

Jessop did not acknowledge him. He kept looking at the mountains as if he expected Kalanu, in the form of a raven, to come down and carry him away. Parker took a step toward him. He was trying to keep calm. He had been in enough classes teaching him to deal with crazy people, and he didn't want to scare him into doing something stupid. At the same time he was really angry at Jessop and trying not to let it show. He remembered the rules.

114

Try not to be belligerent.

Try not to be threatening.

Talk soothingly. Be friendly. Don't invade his space. Be in command of the situation.

"Come on now, Clyde," Parker said. "It's really cold up here. Why don't you come on down and we'll have some coffee. I think there's some chocolate cake in the break room. You like chocolate cake? We could have some coffee and chocolate cake."

Down below his watch commander drove into the yard in one of the shiny new Chevrolets that had only been delivered a day before. The department generally got a limited number of new cars every other year and the new ones had all the bells and whistles.

Just as his watch commander climbed out of his car, Jessop spread his arms out wide and shouted 'Kalanu' and launched himself off the side of the building as if expecting to fly.

He did not.

He went straight down like a rock and smashed against the hood of his commander's new patrol unit.

CHAPTER SIXTEEN

Micki was driving fast along Atlanta Highway, but Tobias could already see the shadows playing along the top of Kalanu Mountain. It would be dark soon. And colder. Sharon Bishop, if she were alive, was going to have to spend another long night on the mountain. His memories of spending nights on the mountain were joyous, but he had a big fire, hot dogs and hamburgers, his grandfather's stories and Matt Trueblood keeping him company. He could not imagine what Sharon Bishop was going through. His heart ached for her, and he tried desperately to think of something else, anything else he could do. It only made his head hurt worse.

He knew there were others out working now. There were other investigators asking questions of the men on Eddie's list, but somehow Tobias knew it was all a waste of time. It was Gus Creel, who had her, and he had her on the mountain.

Micki had to take a detour at the college because there was a wreck on the road ahead. There was another wreck being reported at the county line, and still another on Murphy Road out near Lake Bellman. The roads were getting slick and dangerous, the weather creating an additional need for officers who were already working dangerously long shifts.

The Georgia State Patrol was helping, but they were also stretched thin. All the mountain communities in the area would be having the same issues. It was going to be a long night for everyone.

He was not surprised to see an ambulance in front of the Sheriff's department. Sometimes the county drivers dropped in for coffee during the long shifts. What did surprise him was to see somebody on a stretcher being put into the back by two paramedics. They were not being gentle with the stretcher which meant the person underneath the thin sheet was beyond caring.

In the parking lot they met Owen MacGruder. He stood with his hands in his pocket, watching the ambulance.

"Who?" Tobias said.

"Your friend Jessop. He just took a nose dive off the top of the building. I expect he was waiting for Kalanu to fly him away. Kalanu must have been busy elsewhere."

"How the hell?"

116

"Excellent question. The Sheriff has got everybody who was in the station house tonight in separate interview rooms and we're waiting on that hotshot investigator from the Governor's office."

"You mean Carp."

"Yeah. He's supposed to be on his way. I have a feeling this is going to be really nasty."

"Jack and Gail Mathis were on duty tonight."

"Yeah. Jack was supposed to be running patrol tonight and you know he hates the jail work, but Gail tapped him for the duty when the regular officer called in sick. It's her way of not showing favoritism, so now both of them are on the block."

"Who else?"

"Palmer."

Just hearing the name made Tobias nod. . He knew Palmer well, had tried several times to get him removed from duty. It wasn't that he disliked Palmer. He had worked with people he disliked before. But he knew Palmer was lazy and cut corners. He expected this time Palmer would not walk away.

Owen knew what Tobias was thinking.

"Yeah, I agree. My bet is on Palmer."

There were other cars in the parking lot and he recognized one of them. It was the blue Cadillac SUV that was usually driven by Mason Creel. It was bad news. If Mason Creel was in the building, he was playing politics and it was getting ugly.

Harvey Abercorn's office seemed full of people, but there were only three, but one of them was enormous. Mason Creel weighed in at nearly 300 pounds and most of it was belligerent. He was a second cousin to Miss April Creel, and he had been involved in politics in Kalanu County for as long as anyone could remember. He had been mayor of Mount Rawls for a time and a county magistrate for a time, and now he served as chairman of the county commissioners.

Creel seldom was seen in the company of his cousins, but Tobias always suspected he was involved in a lot of their activities. But it could never be proven. Mason Creel was a sly as a fox.

The other man in the room besides Harvey Abercorn was a slim, tall, distinguished looking man in an expensive suit. He was one of the commissioners who had been constant opponents of Harvey Abercorn. Everything about him reeked of money. Rufus Silverman owned Silverman Real estate and most of the land out around Lake Bellman. He lived in a palatial home on the water's edge. He was a widower and lived with his daughter, Sandra, and her husband and two children, and was probably the most influential politician in the county.

Barry Silverman was his other child.

Between the two of them was a lot of political leverage, a lot of votes, and a longstanding dislike of Tobias, although for different reasons. Mason Creel hated him because Tobias had been arresting members of his family for years. Mason was a fat spider who sat in the center of his political world, sending out threads in all directions. Tobias knew he had been involved in several crimes, but had never been able to prove anything. Lesser members of the family had gone to jail, but Mason had always slithered away. George Silverman disliked Tobias for more personal reasons, a one-time business deal that went sour between the Silverman family and the Atkins family.

"I'm asking for an independent investigation," Rufus Silverman said.

"I've already done that," Harvey said wearily.

"I don't know how a thing like this could happen," Creel said.

"That's what the investigation will find out," Harvey said. "That's why they call it an investigation."

"Don't get smart with me, Abercorn," Creel said.

"You're taking up a lot of space in my office," Harvey said.

"What's that supposed to mean?" Creel said.

"It means unless you have some constructive to say, don't let the door hit you in the ass on the way out."

It showed Tobias how really tired Harvey was. Harvey was usually better at dealing with the political influences and the newspapers. It was his talent. But lack of sleep and the stress was wearing his usually enormous amount of patience very thing.

"Tobias cleared his throat to make himself noticed.

"You," Mason Creel said with a disgusted emphasis.

"What's he doing here? Rufus Silverman asked. "He's not supposed to be involved in any investigations. He's on medical leave."

"He's still on leave," Harvey said.

"So what is he doing here?"

"Yeah." Creel said, "everybody knows he's crazy as a bedbug. He should be home in bed with that pretty wife of his instead of out at the café asking questions." He looked back at Abercorn. "Yeah, I heard about that. You've been looking for Gus."

"We've been looking for Gus for a while now," Harvey said.

"Yeah, but now you're throwing around his name as being involved in this kidnapping. It's a damned lie. It's only because Atkins hates anybody with the name of Creel. It's an obsession with him. It seems like he would have known better."

'I think Gus is involved in this," Tobias said.

"You think!" Creel said. "You already have the kidnapper except now his brains are scattered all over the front pavement."

"Gus is involved," Tobias insisted.

"And you have evidence of this?" Rufus Silverman asked.

"I have evidence that Gus and Clyde Jessop were in jail together. I have proof that Gus met Sharon or had the opportunity to meet her. I'll get more proof before this is done."

"No, you won't," Silverman said, "as of now, you're done with this department."

"That's my decision," Harvey said.

"Not if you read the rules, Sheriff. You are an elected official. Your deputies are not. They are county employees and subject to county laws. Your boy here has been out on medical leave. He's been claiming to be incapacitated and collecting health insurance. Now I find him working as a detective, doing his job. You can't have it both ways. He is either sick or not. If he's not, then there's fraud involved and I think you'll find I'm within my rights to suspend without pay until we investigate."

"He wasn't investigating," Harvey said. "He did me a favor because a little girl's life is at risk."

"Then either way he's through helping," Silverman said. "Send him home. I'm sure his wife misses him."

There was an unpleasant sense in the room that Tobias didn't quite understand. He understood the dislike for him and the political maneuvering but there was something else underneath the surface. It was like everybody in the room, except for Tobias, knew a secret and nobody was telling him.

"I think we can agree to that," Harvey said. "It's time he went home."

"Good," Mason Creel said.

"But I think he's right. I think Gus Creel did take that little girl."

Mason Creel's eyes narrowed.

"If I were you, Mason," Harvey said, "I'd start preparing a speech about how terribly sorry you are that anybody named Creel was involved in this."

"You'd like that, wouldn't you?" Creel said.

"Yes," Harvey said softly. "I think I would."

Harvey had menace in his voice. There was a trace of the old Harvey for a moment, the guy who had worked a patrol zone by himself, the fierce cop inside the smooth politician and it made Mason Creel step back involuntarily.

"I think everyone should take a deep breath," Rufus Silverman said.

Mason Creel nodded. "When this is over, I think we'll have a long meeting the board of commissioners. Maybe it's time we started looking at a county police department. We're getting big enough. The Sheriff's department can watch the jail. Not that you do a great job of that."

"When this is over," Harvey said. "And your cousin ends up getting charged with kidnapping, I doubt you'll be on the commission anymore so we won't have to worry about that. I doubt you could get elected dog catcher."

Mason looked at Rufus Silverman but Silverman did not meet his eyes. Everyone in the room understood the implication. If Gus Creel were guilty, Mason could expect no support from the Silverman side of the commission.

The two men left the office and Harvey breathed a soft sigh. "The problem is they are right, Tobias. There's a dead man who was a kidnapper and a convicted child molester and newspapers are going to make him look like a saint. They'll do anything to make the police look bad."

"We made ourselves look bad," Tobias said. "We had him in our custody and he died."

Sheriff Abercorn gave Tobias a withering look. "You're not helping to ease my mind."

"This is a nasty business," Tobias said. "And I believe there's more involved than just a kidnapping."

"I don't understand," Harvey said.

"I don't either yet. But I don't believe Gus Creel made that phone call."

"If he didn't, who did?"

"It might have been another Creel. It might have been somebody with a serious grudge against the Windfall Project. It might have been somebody looking for kicks. I don't know. But something else is going on."

"You're a lot of help for a trained investigator," Harvey said.

"I've been sick," Tobias shrugged.

…..

Mitchell Carp sat in the break room when they left Harvey's office. He had his shoes off and he was leaning back in one of the flimsy chairs. He looked troubled and tired.

"Back again, Mitch?" Tobias said.

"No rest for the wicked," Mitchell said. He gave Micki an obvious lecherous look. "You wouldn't have any sympathy for a tired old man?"

"I've already warned you to be nice, Carp. I'm not taking the blame if she hurts you."

"It might be worth it," Carp said.

"You're a sick puppy," Tobias said.

"I don't know," Micki said. "He's not such a bad looking sort."

She did it again. The same thing she had done with Barry Silverman up on the mountain. Her face became all smiles. She seemed to become soft, pliable, willing. She leaned her breast into Carp and leaned over and kissed him on his weathered cheek. Carp's face turned very red.

"I think I'd kill you though," she said.

She laughed and changed back into the cold, impassable Cherokee princess, winked at Tobias, and went out of the room. It was a moment before both men could breathe.

"How did she do that?"

"I don't know. I think she's a witch."

"You look lousy, boyo," Carp said.

"Thanks," Tobias answered.

Tobias sipped his coffee. He was tired of stale coffee. He was tired of a lot of things.

"So what happened?" Carp said.

"Clyde Jessop took a nose dive off the roof because of bad police work, and I lost my last chance to talk to him. I wanted to see his face when I told him Gus Creel was Kalanu. I know he would have talked to me then. He would have told me something I could use, damn it."

"You want me to write this report up as incompetent police work?" Carp said.

Tobias shook his head. "I'm angry."

"And you're beat. You should go home and sleep."

"Yeah," Tobias said bitterly. "I sleep in a nice warm bed while that little girl freezes again on top of the mountain."

"Come on, Swede. You've been in the business long enough to know that it's the nature of the beast. You can't save everybody."

"Or anybody," Tobias said bitterly.

"So who was watching Jessop?" Carp asked.

"You interviewing me," Tobias questioned.

"I'm going to be interviewing everybody," Carp said. "Right now I have three officers in separate interview rooms. Two of them have the same names which I find interesting."

"Sergeant Gail Mathis and husband Jack."

122

"It's usually not a good thing to have a married couple on the job. In fact, most police departments prohibit it. The only married couple I ever remember was a lieutenant in Gwinnett County and his wife, but she worked radio dispatch and even that was kind of stressful at times."

"She was on the job first. He came along later. People on the job weren't supposed to date each other, but they managed it. Abercorn wasn't happy when she announced they were going to be married, but they were both good cops. Both of them have a spotless record."

"Until tonight," Carp said. "Are you sure they didn't slip off the job for a little while, maybe out to the cars for a little romantic quickie?"

Tobias shook his head. "Actually, Jack might have been up for the idea, but Gail is pure professional on the job."

"So that leaves the other guy. Deputy Art Palmer."

Tobias looked down at the floor for a moment. "Him?"

"You don't approve?"

"You remember an officer named Wells who used to work for DeKalb? A detective."

"I remember Officer Wells," Carp said. "He was lazy and inefficient and dangerous to others on the job."

"Palmer reminds me of him," Tobias said.

"So you think he's guilty of something," Carp said.

"I don't know. I wouldn't want to influence your investigation."

"Sure you wouldn't," Carp said. He stood up slowly and stretched. He looked almost as tired as Tobias. It had been a long day for all of them.

"Say, you couldn't put in a good word for me, could you? I mean, it would be something to date the daughter of a famous actress."

"She's too young for you, Carp, but I'll put in a good word for you. In fact, I'll tell her everything I know about you."

Carp frowned. "And I thought you were my friend."

.....

Tobias must have fallen asleep because the next thing he knew Micki was gently shaking his shoulder.

"Swede," she said. "Let me take you home."

He straightened up in his chair, felt the muscles of his lower back protesting.

"Not yet," he said. "How long has Carp been away?"

"He's been in the interview room with Jack for an hour," she said.

He shook his head to clear away some of the fog. He picked up his coffee cup but it was cold and he couldn't stand the thought of drinking any more.

"You want something from the machine?" Micki asked.

"No. Carp wants to date you."

"What?"

"I told him he's too old for you, but then you told me you like older men."

"Old, not infirm," she said.

"He's my age," Tobias said.

"But you look much older,' she said.

She grinned at him. She bought a pack of cheese crackers from the machine. For some reason he was irritated by the rattling of the paper as she unwrapped it. He knew the signs. His investigation was stalling, his pain and headaches getting worse.

"Have we heard anything about any of the other names on the list?"

"Nothing. But you didn't expect to, really."

"No," he said. "It's Creel. I know its Creel."

"You've done all anyone can do," Micki said.

"But I can't remember where the Cloud Place is, and if I could remember that, we could find Creel."

"I'm surprised you can remember anything, Swede," Micki said. "You are exhausted."

Jack Mathis stepped into the room and if there was anybody who looked worse off than Tobias, it was Mathis. His shoulders sagged with defeat. His face was pale, his expression miserable.

"Carp give you a hard time?" Tobias asked.

"He wanted to know if we were together when it happened, "Mathis said.

"Together?" Micki asked.

"You know … together."

"Oh," Micki said.

"I didn't see anything, Swede. I didn't know anything. I was by myself in the dungeon. You know Gail. She's not the type to fool around on the job."

"I know," Tobias said.

"But Gail took him upstairs," Mathis said. "What if she left the door open? Sometimes it doesn't lock properly. You know you have to be careful."

"She locked it, Jack."

"Nobody can be sure," Jack Mathis said miserable. "Nobody can."

Jack Mathis was large and blond, muscular. Women thought him good looking but he seemed unaware of it, and he seemed totally devoted to his wife. He was so big that just his physical presence was intimidating, and it took a great deal to shatter his calm demeanor and make him angry. Making him angry was like prodding a stick at a sleeping grizzly. It was not the smartest thing to do. The only person who never seemed intimidated by him was his much smaller wife.

Micki leaned across the table and took his big hands in hers.

"It's going to be all right, Jack," she said. "You know Gail is smart. You know she wouldn't leave the door open. She'd check and double check."

Hope flickered in the big man's eyes.

"It's going to be all right," Micki said again.

Something caught in Tobias's throat and he had to look away. The expression on Micki's face reminded him of her father. Matt Trueblood had a way with people sometimes, a gift of reaching into their souls and calming them.

Carp and Sheriff Abercorn came in for coffee. Both men looked glum and unhappy.

"Owen called," Harvey said. "He says he had a long interview with another cellmate of Gus Creel. He says the book

Creel was reading was "Tales by a Smoky Mountain Campfire."
He said he read it over and over all the time they were cellmates."

"That pretty much tears it then," Tobias said. "It's no doubt
its Creel."

"I've sent word up to Silverman on the mountain,"
Abercorn said. "I'd like to go up myself but now I have this mess
to contend with."

"How's Gail … Sergeant Mathis," Jack asked.

"We've got her statement down," Abercorn said. "Now
we're going to put Palmer under oath, but I already know what
he's going to say. He's already told me once tonight that Jessop
was already in the yard when he went back. He said something that
makes sense. He said Jessop must have been out there a long time
since he found a way to climb up to the bottom ladder. I'm sorry
but that does make sense. That's an eight foot jump. Jessop
couldn't have made that. He had to have time to climb."   Abercorn
put his hand on Jack's shoulder. "I've got tell you, Jack. It doesn't
look good for Gail right now. We all know about that door
sticking. Maybe she got into a hurry. Everybody makes mistakes."

"I don't believe it," Tobias said.

Abercorn looked at Tobias harshly. "You need to get your
ass home. Abby's been ringing the phone off the hook. I keep
telling her I don't know where you are. You've got some
explaining to do."

"Gail locked the door behind her," Tobias said. "She's a
good cop. She wouldn't make a mistake like that."

"Go home," he said.

"Abercorn," Tobias said, as Carp and the Sheriff turned to
leave. "Check by the back door."

"For what?"

"Parker's a smoker. You can smell it on his clothes. Check
around the back door and see if there are any recent cigarette
butts.'

"What would that prove?"

"You're running a skeleton crew tonight. If someone was
smoking back there, it was probably Parker. Are you telling me
that Jessop was running around outside and Parker had the time to
smoke a cigarette."

126

"He'll only say he smoked it later, afterwards," Abercorn said. "And it might be true."

"Check anyway," Tobias said.

"I will," Carp said.

They left to interview Parker. In a few moments Sergeant Gail Mathis appeared in the doorway.

"They're sending me home," she said. "I'm not on suspension. Yet. I expect that's coming."

"Gail," Tobias said.

"Save it, Swede," she said. "I know how things work and I'm not in the mood to talk about it right now. A man is dead, isn't he? No matter what happens, it was on my watch." She looked at Jack. Her face was cold, impassive. Jack had tears in his eyes. "I'm going home."

"I'm going with you," he said.

"No, you're not. You're going back to the dungeon. We're shorthanded tonight. Abercorn is going to need every working officer he can get. You do your job, Jack."

Jack nodded but he didn't take his eyes off his wife until she disappeared down the hallway.

"Try not to worry, Jack,' Micki said.

"Try asking me not to breathe," he said

…..

There was another two hours of interview before Mitchell Carp was finished. Dutifully Jack Mathis had gone back to his post in the dungeon. The watch commander had been called away and the Nun had been called back to work the desk. There was a steady flow of wet, cold officers coming. Two drunks were brought in, a burglar, a man and wife involved in a domestic squabble and also drunk. A ten year old boy sat in the break room for a while until his parents came to fetch him. Tobias was never sure what the boy was there for.

Tobias was almost asleep again when Carp settled down into the chair across from him.

"I feel like you look," he said.

"That bad, huh?" Tobias said. "Are you going to be charging anybody?"

"Not with anything criminal, and there are no real laws against stupidity," Carp said. "By the way, someone had been smoking outside. I checked and it was Palmer's brand."

"So what's his story?"

"Exactly what Abercorn said it would be. He got here. He was asked to escort Jessop down to the cells. He found Jessop in the back yard. The automatic door was wedged open. Jessop was climbing up the ladder."

'How did the back door get opened? It takes a key card to open the door."

"He couldn't explain that one."

"You already know what happened. He was smoking. He forgot to close the door and Jessop went outside as soon as he opened the interview room door."

"I might believe it but I don't know if we have a way of proving it. Just as likely scenario is that Sergeant Mathis put him in the interview room and then didn't lock the door properly, and maybe the back door had already been left open."

"You don't believe that for a second," Tobias said.

"It doesn't matter what I believe," Carp said. "Either way, I don't see how Jessop got to that ladder. That's better than eight foot jump straight up. I don't know how he managed it."

"Let me talk to Palmer," Micki suggested.

There was something in her face that made Tobias shiver. "Not sure another homicide will solve our problems."

128

CHAPTER SEVENTEEN

"I don't know what else to do now," Tobias said. "There's always a place in an investigation where the road runs out. I guess this is it."

"So now I take you home," Micki said. "You look like death warmed over and I'm sure Abby has a few things to say."

"I'm not looking forward to that," he admitted.

"You should have called her. You were only putting off the inevitable."

"There must be something else we can do," he said. "There has to be. That child cannot stay on the mountain another night. It's getting colder all the time and I would bet the snow is already falling higher up. Damn Gus Creel anyway."

Abby's black BMW was parked in the driveway when Micki pulled in. Micki had the car radio turned to a news channel out of Gainesville and the kidnapping and search for Gus Creel was the topic of the hour. There were more searchers volunteering to help, but authorities were warning people to stay home and indoors because an ice storm was on the way. The search on the mountain would certainly soon be hampered because of the weather, and conditions would make the roads treacherous. Both of them sat in silence listening to the weather reports with a dull dread.

"They'll have to call it off soon," Micki said.

"Yes," Tobias said.

Another reporter came on the station and there was no mistaking the voice of Tracy Clavier. The man involved in the kidnapping of Sharon Bishop was believed to have fallen to his death from the roof of the Kalanu County Sheriff's department. The district attorney promises a thorough investigation will be made by an outside agency to determine the fault and proper measures would be taken to see that a thing like this never happens again.

"Poor, sad, twisted little man," Tobias said.

Micki glanced at him, surprised. "You actually feel sympathy for that?"

"I don't know if feeling sorry is the word. I only know nobody starts out to be a child molester, or a murderer, or a thief. Some believe its environment, some genetics. I believe that there is just evil in the world that gets into people sometimes. Call it the devil, if you like."

"The devil made me do it," Micki said, with an almost smile in her voice.

"Sometimes he does," Tobias said.

"You are a strange person, Swede."

"So I've been told."

The front door of the ranch-style brick home opened and Abby stood in the doorway, arms folded across her chest.

"I won't come in," Micki said.

"Probably a good idea," Tobias said.

"I'm certain Abby would not greet me with a friendly smile," Micki said. She looked toward the house and frowned. "Swede, I know you and Dad used to talk about things. I'm not my dad but if you need someone to talk to about anything … just call."

"Thanks," he said.

He had the feeling again that there was something she wanted to say, but she didn't know how to find the words. Finally, he slipped out of the car and walked up to the sidewalk to where Abby waited. She shivered a little in the cold. She wore the quilted blue robe he had bought her on the last Christmas he could remember. She had recently showered because her hair was damp.

He expected accusations, confrontation, and he wouldn't have blamed her.

Instead she said, "Are you all right, Swede?"

"I just have a little headache," he said.

He was not telling the complete truth for his head was pounding and his every muscle felt strained, but for some reason even making a tiny confession irritated him. At first when he had been released from the hospital she had smothered him with care as if her tending his every need would help him heal faster. He had resented not being able to do things for himself, resented feeling like a child under strict supervision, but the problem was he couldn't do a lot of things for himself. And he hadn't recovered quickly and he had grown tired of being her child, and she had grown impatient with being his mother.

Perhaps it was partially the age difference because they were of different generations and he had been kidded a lot about taking a child bride. She was more than twenty years younger, but it had been good in the beginning, before his injury. They had laughed a lot together. Lately, there had been very little laughter.

Abby took his hand and led him into the living room where he sat down on a leather couch. She left and returned with a small blue pill and a glass of water. He hated the pills. They helped his headaches but they also made him feel groggy and confused. In the beginning the doctors had prescribed a stronger dose and it ended up giving him hallucinations. They confused his thinking.

He took the pill because he knew the headache was going to get worse. It had been coming all day and he knew it would finally get so bad that he would want to strike his head against the wall just to give relief.

Abby sat across from him on a flimsy looking chair that had cost more than the couch. Abby liked nice things. She would spend an enormous sum for a chair that was more show than substance. He liked comfortable things.

"That woman shouldn't have dragged you up the mountain," Abby said.

"She didn't drag me," he said. "They thought I could help."

"You can't even dress yourself half the time," she said. "And now you have a headache and you're going to be up sick for most of the night. You should not have gone."

"No," he said.

"You're not that Swede Atkins anymore," she said, "and people have to realize that if you're ever going to get better."

The edge in her voice told him that she didn't believe he was ever going to get better. Sometimes he didn't believe it himself. He leaned his head back. The room was very quiet. He could hear the ticking of a clock somewhere and the sound of a car engine from the street. Their home was on a secluded street at the north end of Mount Rawls, and only a mile from the bank where Abby worked. It was convenient for her but he had not wanted to live in the city. He would have preferred to be living in his grandfather's cabin but it was nearly a forty-minute ride from the city and only accessible by a mile-long, narrow road. At one time it had been the only home on the road. There were several other Alpine type homes built up there now, summer homes for tourists, but still it was quiet and secluded, with a good view of the mountains. Just spending the weekend up there made Abby crazy.

"I'm going to run you a bath," Abby said. "A hot bath always helps you relax.'

The pill was working. He felt a little dreamy. His conversation with Jessop went through his mind. It still bothered him about the Cloud Place. Trying to remember the exact words. "Up the three rivers to the Cloud Place." What in the hell was the Cloud Place? He was sure it was where Gus Creel was with the girl, but he was equally sure he had never heard of it. It was something twisted in Jessop's mind, maybe words he had gotten wrong.

Cloud Place.

Place of Clouds, maybe.

Fluffy place? Sky place? Someplace with clouds? Changing the words around maybe? A place of the clouds? It frustrated him. There was something, something just at the edge of his consciousness but it wouldn't become clear.

Abby returned. He was in the dream state now, his mind dull. At least the headache was only a slight sensation of pressure and his muscles were moving loosely again. Abby led him docilely into the bathroom and undressed him. His clothes on the floor, he stepped into the steaming, soapy bath and settled down. He leaned back and closed his eyes.

The Cloud Place.

It had to be somewhere high up on Kalanu, but high up would mean cold and the child had few clothes. Was Gus Creel keeping her warm and dry? Was she dead already?

Silverman was probably right. The child was dead already and Gus Creel would eventually be caught and sent to jail and there was no point in him worrying like a dog worrying a bone.

Crazy Gus Creel. No rhyme or reason to his thinking patterns. Tobias had arrested him four times in eight years, mostly

132

for assault and mostly because Creel got drunk and crazy. Perhaps all the years of drinking had destroyed his brain cells. Maybe he was just crazy now, and he didn't have to be drunk.

He thought he was Kalanu, the raven, the witch.

And if he hadn't killed that little girl by now, he was going to. It was a matter of time.

What had Jessop said? She was the chosen one. Chosen for what? Some sort of ritual sacrifice. There was no question Gus Creel was involved, and Tobias doubted that Creel was anywhere near sane anymore. When Lilly Creel had picked up the shovel and sent Tobias into oblivion, Creel was already showing signs of being mentally ill. Perhaps he had always been, even back in high school when his savage line backing skills had often reduced the players on other teams to tears.

Abby returned. She knelt by the tub with a washcloth. Her hand was gentle as she rubbed his chest and around his neck. He looked into her face. There were tears on her cheeks.

"Oh, what they did to you," she said softly. "What they did to you, Swede."

"It's all right, Abby," he said.

She was crying, soft, choking sobs and he stood up and took her in his soapy arms and held her close to him. She cried for a long time, putting her face in his shoulder. She cried until he started shivering with the cold and she drew back. She grabbed tissue and blew her nose.

"I must look a mess," she said.

"You're beautiful, Abby," he said, and he kissed her and then drew her into his arms again.

"No, Swede,' she said softy. "No, you're not well enough."

He wondered how well a man had to be. He kissed her again and she responded only a moment and then she pushed him away. There was something in her face he didn't recognize, something that seemed almost like guilt. He had seen such looks before, and he felt a darkness inside himself that hadn't been there before.

"It's all right, Abby," he said.

"No, it's not," she said. "It's never going to be all right."

She helped dry him off and they went into the bedroom. She took off the robe but she wore a dark flannel nightgown with little sex appeal. It was her gown for cold winter nights and her gown that said, "Don't touch me; I'm not in the mood."

She sat up in the bed with him and they watched one of the late night shows, and finally he heard her breathing deeply. He used the remote and turned off the television and lay in silence and tried to sleep himself but sleep wouldn't come.

His mind was too full of desperation and cloud places. He finally could stand it no longer and he slipped quietly out of bed and left the bedroom. He went into the small room off the front that had served as his home office. He had not been in the room for a while. It smelled slightly musty. He turned on the desk lamp and searched his small collection of hardback books, mostly criminal investigation techniques and legal cases, until he found his grandfather's book. He went to his desk and sat. He started at the beginning of the story of Kalanu and read through it twice. It was frustrating. No matter how many times he read it, there was no mention of a cloud place.

He leaned back. He wished the old man were with him now. His grandfather would know the answer.

"Where is it?" he said out loud.

Somewhere on the mountain, if she wasn't already dead, was a terrified child, and all he needed to do to rescue her was remember, but he couldn't.

He closed his eyes and once again went over Jessop's exact words. He had trouble remembering things but he had spent so many of the past few hours trying to remember the exact words and it came back to him easily. He could see his face, his form, taste the horribly bad coffee, hear the sounds of a tree limb moving in the wind and brushing the outside of the tent.

Creepy little man sitting across from him in the folding camp chairs, hands nervously twisting, eyes evasive.

"Kalanu took her," Jessop said. "He swooped down off the mountain, and took her across the three rivers to the cloud place."

But there was no cloud place any place in his grandfather's writings, nor in any history of the mountain he had ever read, or on any map he knew of. Perhaps Jessop had gotten the words wrong but he couldn't think of anything else that fit.

"He swooped down off the mountain, and took her across the three rivers to the cloud place."

A direction of some kind. Across the three rivers.

Three rivers, Tobias thought.

And then he said softly, "Damn."

There, all along. It wasn't hidden in some kind of code. Jessop had given him directions, had told him what he wanted to know and he had been too blind or stupid to see it. Excitement burned in him, the kind of excitement he had not felt in a long time. Matt Trueblood used to laugh at him in such moments. Matt Trueblood could read his expressions, would know when he had worked out the answer, and he would laugh and say in his best Basis Rathbone voice, "The game's afoot, Watson."

There was no Matt Trueblood to celebrate with him anymore, or make references to fictional detectives in his sardonic tone. There was only a scattering of ashes on the mountain, and memories.

"The game's afoot, Watson."

Lord, he missed his friend.

He heard Abby's footsteps and looked up to see her in the doorway.

"What do you think you're doing?"

"It's not the cloud place," he said. "It never was. It was something else entirely."

"I don't know what you're talking about," she said.

"I didn't tell Hattie what he said. I should have. She would have known immediately that it wasn't about a cloud place. I should have told her exactly what Jessop said."

"So go call her now," Abby suggested. "Hell, it's only a little after midnight. I'm sure she won't be asleep like normal people."

'I have to go," he said.

"You have to go," Abby repeated his words tonelessly.

"I have to see her and Micki, and I have to get people looking."

135

"And you can't do it on the phone. And it can't wait until morning?"

"I have to do it my way, Abby," he said.

Tension was making him feel his headache again. His muscles were also tensing up.

"This is so stupid," Abby said. "You don't need to do this yourself. Call the Sheriff. Call that Indian woman. Just give them your information and let them handle it. You're a sick man, Swede, and your head is hurting right now. I can see it in your eyes."

"That little girl can't wait any longer."

"All right," Abby said. "I'll throw on a coat and drive you over there. Do you think you can tie your own shoelaces in the meantime?"

He walked gingerly into the bedroom behind Abby. She went into the bathroom and slammed the door. He almost couldn't tie his own shoelaces. It was painful. His muscles were really cramping up now, and he knew he would not be able to walk ten feet without help. He knew he shouldn't do it but he found the bottle of pills and shook one more out into his hand and swallowed. He also stuffed the bottle down into his pocket. It was a short-term fix because the muscle spasms would come back with a vengeance, but it would help for a while. He only hoped the hallucinations would stay away.

The pill helped almost immediately. He was able to pull on his trousers and shirt and he chose a heavy coat from the closet. He also pulled down a black box from the top shelf and took out the ancient 38 police special he had carried as a new detective. They all carried fancier weapons now but this old pistol felt comfortable to him, and it was all he had except a shotgun. He loaded the pistol with five rounds and put it in his jacket pocket. He probably wouldn't need it. There was no reason to think he would.

And he knew it was both stupid and dangerous to be walking around with a loaded pistol in his pocket when he was on medication.

A couple of times his better sense tempted him to put it back in the closet but then Abby came out of the bathroom and he couldn't put it up in front of her.

Abby was angry. It showed in her face and the stiffness of her body as she led him out to the car. It had gotten colder and he shuddered as cold icy fingers went down his spine. The promised ice storm was coming. He could taste it on his lips.

Snow was better than ice.

Snow was manageable but the black ice would tear down power lines and make the roads treacherous, and make deputies workloads unmanageable. It would also make searching on the mountain impossible.

Time was quickly running out for Sharon Bishop.

CHAPTER EIGHTEEN

In the front of Hattie's apartment, Abby pulled into the curb.

"I'll leave you here," she said abruptly. "That Inidan woman can bring you home."

"Abby ... " he said.

"I have to go to work in the morning and I've lost enough sleep as it is."

He knew her well enough to know she wasn't intentionally being cruel, but he recognized a sharp finality. She was hurt and tired and worried. He expected he was crossing over a bridge he could not return from, and there was no time to talk it through.

He walked up the sidewalk to the apartment house. Hattie opened the door before he reached it.

"I thought I was going to beat on it for a while to wake you up," he said.

"I was grading papers," she said. "I saw you through the window. You're alone?"

"Abby called Micki for me. She's coming. I didn't have your number."

"It's unlisted. I guess we should have thought of that, but then I didn't expect any midnight visits."

Mad Hattie looked softer, prettier, in the pale light. Her hair was down to her shoulders. She wore a blue quilted robe. Her apartment did not have the clutter of her space at work. It was neat, clean, efficient looking. She had a desk by the window. It was covered with stacks of folders.

"I was drinking coffee. You want some?"

"Yes, please."

He sat on the couch. The pills were really starting to kick in because he wasn't feeling any soreness and he was able to move without wincing. But he was struggling to keep his mind clear. He didn't want to fall into the dreamy state. All the way over he had been counting numbers. He knew he could slip into the half-awake state and his head would stop hurting, but he kept fighting it. His head would have to hurt as long as his muscles were relaxed and he could move.

He would pay for it later, but now he needed to keep away the sleep and hallucinations.

Abby brought him a cup of coffee and settled down beside him on the couch.

"You remembered something?" Hattie said.

He started to answer and the doorbell rang. It was Micki. She didn't want coffee and she settled into the chair across from them. She had not changed from her earlier outfit. He still wondered where she kept her gun. She looked at him curiously.

"It wasn't the cloud place," he said. "It never was. I focused on it so much that I didn't hear everything Jessop said."

"What else did he say?" Micki asked.

"He said Kalanu took the girl across the three rivers to the cloud place. I should have been concentrating on the three rivers. I should have told you exactly what he said, Hattie."

"Yes," she said.

"What am I missing?" Micki said.

"Because I should have been thinking about the three rivers crossing," he said. "I don't remember such a place but I'm sure I'm right. I'm sure I've heard of it. That's why I came back to Hattie. If anyone knows of a place on the mountain where there are three rivers crossing, you do."

Hattie shook her head. "You're still wrong."

"Why?"

"Because Three Rivers isn't the name of a place. It's the name of a man."

Something flickered in his memory, some distant pattern of sitting by the fire and his grandfather talking about the crazy white man who came to the mountain even before people started settling it, the man who collected plants.

"The plant stealer," Tobias said.

"Yes, the Cherokees called him that sometimes. But they gave him the official name of Three Rivers Crossing. His real name was Charles Bailey but he visited the mountain in the early years, and often. He wrote down a lot of what he saw and because of him, we know a great deal about the early life of the first settlers in the area. He became friends with the Cherokee and they gave him the name Three Rivers. But what he really is known for his maps. He was one of the first who mapped Kalanu and a part of what we now call the Appalachian Trail. He spent a lot of long summers living alone up on the high places of Kalanu. He built a cabin up there." She stopped. Her face grew animated and she leaned over and touched Tobias on the knee. "I should have remembered. We both should have remembered. One of your grandfather's stories was about Three Rivers. I quote, "Charles Bailey, Three Rivers, built a cabin so high up that it was in the clouds."

"The Cloud Place," Micki said. "The home of Three Rivers."

"The cabin of Charles Bailey," Hattie said. "And we know exactly where it was."

"The cabin is long gone," Tobias said, "but he built it in a historical place. Some people believe the Cherokee were the first people on the mountain and that they have developed through the years, but others believe there were an older people there first, another civilization and not just ancestors of the Cherokee. But if it was Cherokee or some other peoples, there's a place on Kalanu where they left evidence behind. The area where Charles Bailey built his cabin has several rock drawings."

"So you think this is where Gus Creel is hiding," Micki said. "Where he has the girl?"

"It can't be anywhere else," Tobias said. "I'm sure of it."

"So where is it? Do you have a map, Hattie? Can we get deputies up there?"

Hattie shook her head. "You can't get them up there in a hurry. It's almost inaccessible except for a few overgrown trails. I haven't even been up there in a few years. But it's also on the other side of the mountain from where everyone is searching. It would take a full day to hike there."

"We can't wait that long," Tobias said. "We're already out of time."

"Can I land my helicopter somewhere near there?" Micki said.

Hattie thought for a moment. "Yes, I think there might be. A couple of years ago an archeological group from some college did some digging in the area. I don't think they found much of anything but they were up there a couple of weeks. Your father kept them supplied so there must have been a place to put the helicopter down nearby. I saw a few of the group and they didn't look like the hiking type."

"Have you got a map?" Micki asked.

Hattie located an old map in her back bedroom and they spread it out on the kitchen table. Micki studied it intensely for a moment. Finally, she put her finger down on a spot.

"It has to be there. It's the only place flat enough for a helicopter to land."

"It's still a good hike to where you want to be," Hattie pointed out.

"It's got to be there," Micki insisted.

"It's also going be overgrown after two years. Your father probably had it cleared off some beforehand."

"And your father was capable of flying a chopper through the eye of a needle," Tobias pointed out.

"If you don't think I'm good enough, you don't have to go," she said irritably.

"Go with you," Hattie said, alarm in her voice. "He can't go. He can't possibly go. Look at him. He doesn't look as if he could make another step."

"I'm going," Tobias said.

"But I thought you'd get some deputies or some of the Army people?"

"There's not enough time," Micki said. "I was listening on the way over here and the storm's coming in and there's a terrible accident on the scenic highway. All the deputies who aren't involved in the search are working traffic. I'll get hold of Abercorn and tell him what we know, but we'll get no help from Silverman. The man is an idiot. But deep down I know Swede is right about this, and Abercorn will know it, too."

"Look at him," Hattie said. "He can barely stand. He won't be able to keep up with you."

"He'll have to do his best," Micki said.

"Isn't there any other way?" Hattie said.

"I wish there was," Tobias said. "Believe me, I do. I don't want to go up there, but if we don't go, Sharon might die. Hell, she might be dead already."

"But you've still got to try?" Hattie asked.

"It's who I am," Tobias answered.

CHAPTER NINETEEN

Micki was on the phone to the station as she drove toward the airport. It was all bad news.

"Abercorn's not available," she said. '"Another accident on the scenic highway has a couple of fatalities. The State Patrol is out there and all the deputies are blocking up the routes. Looks like we're on our own."

"How about soldiers," he said.

"Silverman's still on the mountain, but it's pretty bad weather up there. It's really starting to come down. I doubt he'll help even if he does believe our story."

It was wet and cold and inky black when they rolled the helicopter out to the hangar. Micki had done a preflight check inside where it was warmer, and now she scrambled up into the cockpit, turned the lights on, and started the engines. He climbed in beside her a lot slower. Through the ghostly glare of lights he could see snow flurries.

"It's kind of dangerous to fly in this kind of weather," he said.

"Yes. Only an idiot would do it."

Tobias started to respond, but then just shook his head. Micki followed the same procedure as before, except this time he could see only darkness below as the helicopter lifted off. Fortunately, he could a dim light in the east and he knew the sun was coming up. His stomach churned and his throbbed as she turned the helicopter upward, and once again he knew she was skimming the tops of trees he could not see. He clutched the seatbelt tightly, closed his eyes. He felt as if they were moving faster than they had moved that morning. The helicopter was shaking a little more in the wind. More than once the lights caught the glare of more snow falling.

"Be nice to be home by the fire," Micki commented.

"Be nice to be almost anywhere else," he said.

"Imagine how Sharon is feeling right now," she said.

He could imagine, and his empathy for her was the only thing that could have made him get into a helicopter on a night like this. If she was alive, she would be terrified. If she were not alive, they were risking their lives for nothing. Gus Creel would be caught sooner or later.

The problem was, they couldn't take the risk.

The snow came harder. The sun was starting to show through brightly, but the snow was still blocking his vision. It was riding in a white cloud. He couldn't see how Micki could see anything, but she was somehow managing to keep from crashing.

He felt it when she started down, his stomach jumping.

"What?" He said.

"I'm going to see if I can shame him into helping," she said.

She put it down by the other helicopter and left the motor running. The other helicopter was covered with a light snow and so was the tent. It was building up on the ground. Tobias's feet crunched as he made his way to the tent.

Inside was warm from two camp stoves. There was nobody around but Barry Silverman. He was in dungarees and a T-shirt, seated by a camp stove, and sipping coffee. He didn't get up when they came in.

"You came up here in that mess," he said. "I'm impressed, but it was a stupid thing to do. Can I offer you both a little nip?"

There was more than coffee in the cup. Silverman was not completely sober.

"What I would like is a couple of deputies or some of your soldiers," Micki said. "Preferably armed. We think we know where Gus Creel is."

"You think you know where he is," Silverman said. "But you don't know. Nobody knows. He could be anywhere on this damned mountain."

"We are pretty sure we know, and we need some help. We're flying up there."

"In the chopper," Silverman said, "in weather like this? You'll kill yourselves."

"We'll get there," Micki said. "Now how about getting on the phone and getting us some help."

He shook his head. "There's no help for you. The Sheriff started pulling his deputies off the mountain a couple of hours ago.

My guys are either holed up in shelters or on the way back down the mountain in trucks. It's too late."

"Then you come," Micki said. "You can follow me in your bird."

"I'm not that crazy," he said.

"I kind of figured that would be your answer," Micki said.

"And I'm not going to let you go," he said.

"What?"

"It is too dangerous. I'm in charge of this operation and I'm not going to have you crashing on the mountain and then we have to rescue you. So you'll stay here until the weather clears."

"We're going," Micki said.

Silverman made a mistake. He put his hand on Micki's shoulder and a moment later found himself sitting on his tailbone on the dirt. He started to get up but something in her face stopped him. It was the same look Tobias had seen on her face when she had put Bubba Creel down at the café. There was something very savage beneath her surface, something quick and violent and dangerous.

Tobias followed her back to the helicopter. Her face was set in grim determination as they lifted off again. At least there was enough light to see now, but a moment later Tobias started wishing it was dark again. He thought she came close to the trees before. Now it seemed like she was daring the trees to get out of her way.

"He was right, you know," Tobias said. "They may end up having to rescue us."

"He's a jackass," Micki said.

I agree, but he still might be right."

"I'll get us there," Micki said fiercely.

"How about getting us back?" He asked.

"One thing at a time," she said.

He looked out of the side of the helicopter and he could see the ground again. He could see the water, a long, snakelike creek winding through the mountain, and he realized she was following the river. To do it, she had to be low, but it was a little scary to to skimming the tops of trees.

Hell, it was very scary.

Somehow she got Abercorn on the radio. Abercorn's voice kept fading out but he got most of the conversation. He heard Abercorn curse and curse again and there was a promise he would get somebody, somehow, started in their direction."

"And do me a favor," Micki said.

"What?"

"You tell Silverman if that little girl dies because he was too drunk and stupid to help, that I'm going to come back and do a rain dance on his head."

Abercorn chuckled and rang off.

"Do you know a rain dance?" Tobias asked.

"Shut up."

"Do you wear some kind of beaded costume when you do it?"

"I said shut up, I'm concentrating."

Tobias had been on some really scary helicopter rides in Vietnam, but he had never been on a ride such as Micki took him. The lightweight helicopter shook in the wind and at times she was almost touching the ground, skimming over thin narrow trails and creeks. He didn't think it was possible. A tree limb broke off against a side window. He saw a hairline crack. He looked out the window at the ground.

"I could jump out and walk from here," he said.

The trees got thicker and she had to pull the helicopter up again. She was still close enough to see the water. He started recognizing features of the terrain. With a sigh, he realized they were close. They passed over what looked like an old tin shed and she brought the helicopter around again until they were hovering over a cleared off area. There was high grass and scrub pine growing in the clearing and trees looked dangerously close. These were old trees with thick, knotty branches that could easily rip apart the thin skin of the chopper.

"Not much room," he said.

"I can bring it down," she said.

She tried. She dropped the helicopter like a rock between two trees and he felt the jerk as branches caught and tore away. He heard her soft "damn" as she pulled the helicopter back up again, the flimsy shell jerking in the wind and snow. And there was a new

146

sound, like a motor grinding somewhere, flimsy metal rubbing together.

"Let's try this again," she said.

Down once more between the trees, like a hummingbird searching for just the right nectar, but a hummingbird with hydraulics for power, and metal aluminum for skin that tore easily. She bought it in almost sideways, in a position he never dreamed a helicopter could manage. This time the rapidy turning blades hit a tree solidly and they bounced up and everything started ripping away. Metal shrieked as it tore and the smell of fuel oil was almost overpowering, and they somehow tore free of the trees and dropped to the ground like a gunshot quail.

"Out," Micki yelled.

He knew without being told, the fuel oil dripping from the side to the ground, and he tore at his seat belt. He couldn't get it undone and looked up to see Micki, her face twisted in the same savage grimace, a long, thin blade in her hand. He thought foolishly for a moment she was going to cut him, but she sliced through the fabric belting and pushed him out of the helicopter door. He hit the ground hard and she hit on top of him. Her hand gripped his arm and he felt her sinewy strength as she practically jerked him to his feet.

"Now run," she shouted.

They ran. The hill they were on had a slight incline and they were over it in a few minutes and practically falling downwards. The explosion was still close enough to throw them both forwards on their faces and close enough for Tobias to feel the searing heat. He wasn't sure he was in one piece, but he gingerly sat up. Nothing seemed to be broken. Micki was already up, rubbing her ankle.

"I think I might have twisted my ankle a little," she said. She looked at the hill at the flames still showing from the burning helicopter. "I think we might have hit a tree."

"You think?"

.....

Later, Jack Mathis would not remember Sheriff Harvey Abercorn ever stopping for a stop sign, or a red light, or even

147

putting on the brakes, on the thirty minute drive from the station to the old logging road on Kalanu. The ride up to the staging area was even more harrowing. The road had been driven up and down a lot during the day and had cut furrows in the grass and dirt that were filling up with ice and snow. The sludge made driving doubly dangerous and there were a few places he thought the jeep was going to slide off the mountain into the abyss below. He breathed a sigh of relief when Abercorn brought the vehicle to a sliding stop in front of the tent. Inside they found three soldiers around the campfire and Barry Silverman stretched out on a folding cot snoring. The smell of alcohol was strong.

"Nobody answering the phones or radio," Abercorn said.

A sleepy looking specialist turned from the heater and gave Abercorn a guilty look. The young specialist looked about fifteen and cold and exhausted.

"Sorry, but nothing's working. The radios or cell phones."

Abercorn took a deep breath. "What's your name, son?"

"I'm specialist Charles, sir."

"Well, Charles, do you think you can get your Colonel up. I need to talk to him."

Charles shook his head. "I'm sorry, sir. We tried when we came in. He's out of it."

"Then who's in charge right now?"

Charles looked sheepish. "I don't know, sir."

"Well, go and find somebody," he said.

Charles didn't look he liked the idea of going back out into the cold, but it was warming a little and he put on his heavy coat and left the tent. Abercorn turned to Mathis.

"Jack, I hate to ask this, but we're all tired. When that young man gets back with whoever is now in charge, I want you to round up all the deputies up here and all the soldiers who are willing, and start up the mountain. From here, it's normally about a five hour trip to the side of the mountain where Swede is going. I doubt if they have reached there yet even in a helicopter and it will take her a while to land, if she can. But I'm sure Swede is right about this. He's not often wrong. Gus Creel has that girl up there and this will be our last chance. And Jack …?"

"Yes, sir."

"Take some medics along with you. I think they'll be needed."

The young specialist returned with a tall, thin major named Tully.

"Your colonel's drunk," Abercorn said bluntly, "and I don't have time to sober him up and I don't have the authority to order you to do anything, but I've got two people up on the mountain looking for that little girl. They're pretty sure they know where she is. I need to get some people moving in their direction and I need them moving an hour ago."

"No problem, sir," Major Tully said. "I'll go myself. I've hiked this mountain a few times and it's familiar to me."

"And Major, this guy you're looking for is a dangerous man," Abercorn said. "I wouldn't take a lot of chances with him."

"Understood," Major Tully said.

"My deputy will also go along," Abercorn said.

"No problem."

At that moment the ground shook almost like an earthquake, and all of them staggered like drunken men. Abercorn felt himself lurching forward as the ground trembled beneath his feet. Jack Mathis caught him before he fell. Behind him a bright orange flame rushed to the sky. Even though it was miles away Abercorn fancied he could feel the heat. A moment later he heard the explosion.

CHAPTER TWENTY

He was a mile away, sitting hunched over a small flickering fire. He was not cold. He felt little anymore, not the cold or the pain of his broken fingers He had broken the fingers only that morning when he slipped and fell on some rocks. He didn't care. He knew his time was getting close. It was his time of revelation, his time of sacrifice. The snow swirled around him and he stuck out his tongue and tasted it. Some part of his brain remembered his childhood, the joy of being out in the early snow. Some years passed without snow, except for higher altitudes. It always snowed in the high places on the mountain.

When the explosion came, it seemed to rock the mountain and he looked up to see a burst of flames high above the trees almost like the mountain was giving him a signal.

He had no idea what had happened, and didn't care. He was Kalanu, spirit of the mountain.

And it was his time.

.....

The snow came, thick and swirling around them, mixed with ash from the still burning helicopter. There was no snow in Vietnam, but the smells were the same. Tobias tasted blood in his mouth and knew he had bitten the inside of his lip.

"The ice made the controls freeze up," Micki said. "I could have brought it down otherwise."

"You brought it down," Tobias said.

"I mean, without all the explosions and fire and stuff," she said.

He looked at her with a disbelieving expression. She was smiling. At that moment he felt a connection with her he had not felt until then. He remembered it so often worked the same way in combat. A guy you hated suddenly became your best friend overnight once the shooting started.

"At least the fire will be a good beacon to people trying to find us," he said.

"Are we in serious trouble?" Micki asked.

"We are truly in a mess, but Abercorn knows where we are and I'm sure he's already got people moving toward us. The temperature is still dropping, but we've both got insulated clothing and fortunately neither of us is badly injured, so it could be a lot worse. The best thing for us is to keep moving."

"So let's go find that girl," Micki said. "She's got to be worse off than we are."

Tobias winced as he took his first step. He recognized the signs. He had an increasing tightness in his lower back that would soon spread down his legs. His legs would start to feel incredibly heavy and then itchy. Eventually he would be unable to move. This time would be the same unspeakable agony he had felt many times before. He put his hand in his pocket and felt the comforting reassurance of his pill bottle. He also felt the bulky weight of his heavy pistol.

"Micki," he said.

"Yes."

"Did you bring a gun?"

"Now is a fine time to be asking me that," she said. "Of course."

He studied her for a moment. "Where?"

"If I told you that, you'd have to marry me and you've had enough wives."

He wasn't sure if she was kidding.

"Listen to me, Micki. If something happens to me, don't take any chances with Creel. He always had a mean streak, but this goes far beyond anything I've ever known him to do. He's got to be really crazy this time. Don't try and talk to him. Don't try and help him. Just shoot him, and keep shooting him until he's dead."

""Nothing is going to happen to you," she said.

"Just shoot him,' he insisted.

"All right," she said.

She led the way. She didn't look cold. She had on a light weight green field jacket that was form fitted, and she had changed her boots for green, waterproof field boots resembling ones he had worn in Vietnam. She did limp slightly on her ankle, but she was still as quick and agile as a mountain goat. He lumbered along like an overweight boar, gasping for breath. He fingered the pill bottle.

He thought of the hike before them, the trail snaking upwards across fallen trees and frozen creeks and ice-slippery mud.

No, he thought. It was still too soon for the pills.

He managed another hundred feet before he was forced to stop and catch his breath. Micki came back to him, her body language showing her impatience. Snow came harder, turning the world around them into a wall of impenetrable white. Green pine trees were already beginning to bend with heavy snow.

"Just one foot ahead of the other, Marine," Micki said. "Isn't that how it goes? Weren't you guys supposed to be the elite?"

"I'm coming," he said.

"Just one foot ahead of the other," she said.

And that was what he tried to do. One foot ahead of the other, sliding on the ice-slippery mud, hitting his knee on broken branches, kicking his toes against the rocks, and always ahead of him, the lithe form of Micki moving almost as if she was dancing around the obstacles.

At the first creek he had to stop and catch his breath. He did not sit for he knew he would not get up again. His lungs felt as they were on fire. Micki came back to him again, and this time her face showed sympathy.

"We're not making good time," she said. "We have to hurry."

"I know," she said.

"Seconds count," she said.

"I know, damn it," Tobias said.

"I'm going to go ahead," she said.

He knew it was inevitable, knew he could not keep up. Every part of his mind and soul screamed that it was wrong for them to separate, but he knew he was reaching the limit of his endurance.

He felt like crying out of hurt, anger and frustration.

"You shoot him if you see him," he said. "Like the old west. Shoot, if you see him."

"I will," she said, but he knew she wouldn't.

It wasn't the normal human reaction. People needed to talk, to be pushed into the corner where they had no choice to fight. It was not natural for most people to take out a pistol and just shoot into the body of another human being. It was a good thing that most normal people were like that, but this time she needed to shoot.

"I'll be right behind you, Micki," he said.

She nodded and she turned and disappeared into the curtain of white. He was careful crossing the creek bed, careful not to slip into the chilled water. He started up the other side. He was trying to remember the path, where it turned and went upward and how far it was.

A half mile or maybe a mile. It was so long ago. He and his grandfather and Matt Trueblood. He and Matt had run on ahead, and there was no pain, no hurting, only the glorious freedom of being young and strong.

One foot ahead of the other.

Get into the rhythm. What she had said about the Marines was true. They might have taught him nothing else but they taught him to march with pain, to walk up and down mountains, in the rain and mud, to carry more than his body weight, to find somehow that last spark of energy and strength to make the last mile.

He managed another hundred yards and his breath was coming in tortured gasps. Cold air burned his lungs. He looked down at his feet, panicked a little because he wasn't sure he was the trail anymore. But it had to be the trail because the hanging limbs and brush made it impossible to wander off. He took another step. It was sheer agony, muscular spasms up and down his legs and a feeling of nausea. Another step. One leg in front of the other. Just keep walking

He went twenty steps and stumbled over a tree limb and fell. He had trouble getting up. He had to plant one foot flat on the ground with his knee up. He pressed all his weight on the back of the raised leg and forced himself to his feet again. Just another step. Then one more.

The trail narrowed and it was still going straight up. The Kala wind was tormenting him, and wet snow was sliding down the neck of his jacket. He walked another quarter of a mile and then he stumbled again.

153

A tree limb jammed into his cheek, a sharp branch scraping and drawing blood. This time he thought he might not be able to get up.

And then the cramps started.

They started in his toes, tightening up so fiercely that it took his breath away, and it moved up to his calves in quivering, contracting spasms that went beyond any pain he had known before, not even when the Vietnamese sniper had put a bullet into his shoulder. He felt if he could stand, his muscles would relax, but he couldn't get off his knees.

Then he thought of Micki on the mountain facing Gus Creel alone and he gave a cry of rage and pushed to his feet with every ounce of strength remaining. He stayed for a second only, wavering like a tree being felled by a lumberjack, and then he dropped to his knees again and he knew he was not going to get up without help.

He reached into his pocket and took out the bottle of pills. He had already taken past his limit. He knew his reaction would not be good, but he also knew it was his only hope. He had overdosed before, and the Sheriff's deputies had brought him home. They had found him singing hymns at the top of his lungs, badly, in the church in his underwear. It was a thing of amusement in the city for a while, but Abby had not been amused.

Abby was seldom amused by anything anymore.

He shook out two in his hand, and then a third. The bottle was empty. He put the bottle back into his pocket. He lifted the pills to his mouth. His hand trembled. Two of them fell into the dirt and he had to search in the dirt to find them. He finally clutched them tightly and pressed them between his lips. He was still reluctant, but he had no choice. He would freeze if he didn't move, and he would be no help for Micki.

He had a dull, dread sense of futility. He didn't think he was going to be much help anyway. Gus Creel was up there waiting somewhere. He could sense him. And he was crazy, and Micki would not shoot first.

But then, as if making a liar out of him, he heard a shot, muted by the snow and distance, but definitely a shot.

Just a single shot.

It told him Micki had found Gus Creel, and he closed his eyes, hoping for more, but no other shots came. And he knew in his heart Micki was in serious trouble because one shot would not stop the insanity of Gus Creel.

CHAPTER TWENTY ONE

In the Cloud Place Micki Trueblood found the child.

She moved faster without Swede tagging alone, but she also missed his presence. There was something comfortable and sturdy, having Swede along. An Aikido instructor had once told her to always watch the eyes because the eyes gave warning of movement and intention, but in Swede's eyes was an unfathomable sadness. He had seen too much of the dark side of life and it showed.

But he was man to depend on, a man with a conscious. Her father had told her that, and she sensed her father felt closer than a brother to him.

She moved quickly, but not so quick that she was unaware of the sounds around her. She was watching for Gus Creel, or any sign of him. The sounds she heard were of branches rubbing together, of snow falling in clumps, of cracking tree branches, and the movement of some small animal.

She knew somehow she would hear his breathing first.

As she jogged, she eased down the zipper on her waterproof jacket and made sure she had easy access to her pistol. She thought of Swede's advice, to shoot first and ask questions later. She hoped it wasn't necessary.

She crossed over another creek, the third one and from the few directions she had gotten, she knew she was close. The trail veered to the right up ahead and then the trail widened and she found herself standing on a sort of plateau. On three sides, the ground cut sharply away and beyond the trail narrowed again and went upwards.

But in the middle of the plateau someone had built a crude lean-to and in the lean-to she could see a cot and someone covered with blankets. Her heart beat faster as she hurried to the lean-to and looked down at Sharon Bishop. Sharon Bishop's eyes were open, but she was shivering and her lips were slightly blue.

"I wet myself," she said. She was crying. "I couldn't help it. I had to go.

"It's all right, darling," she said. "It's time to go home."

She found the link of rusty chain and what seemed like a steel anchor driven into the ground. She tried pulling it up, but it wouldn't budge an inch. In desperation, she searched for something she could use as a pry bar and found only one solid piece of wood that looked like it might work. She dug around it with her fingers and used her knife to sharpen the point of the wood. She used another piece of wood as a fulcrum and tried to work the metal pike out of the floor. It moved an inch but then settled back.

She tried again. Her fingers were getting cold and she blew on them and tried another time. This time the spike came up slightly, but the wood splintered.

She started desperately searching for another piece of wood to use. Or anything else. She smelled him before she heard Sharon Bishop gasp. The smell was strong, almost overwhelming. It was the small of wood smoke and sewer pipes and sweat. She turned her head and saw him standing only a few feet from her. He was nearly naked and she had not expected him to be so big and hairy. She didn't think she'd ever seen a bigger man. And here was no fat on him anywhere. His naked chest was like hardwood. He did not seem effected by the cold.

"I am Kalanu," he roared. "And you are trespassing on my mountain."

"And I am Princess Rain on your Parade," she said, and drew out her pistol and shot him.

.....

Tobias was feeling very pleased with himself. He knew he could have gotten off his knees if he wished, but he was more comfortable where he was. Snow flurries swirled around his head, and he was half smiling. He thought it might be a good idea to stretch out on the ground and sleep for a while. He could restore his energy.

There would be time to help Micki after his nap

"You need to get up," Matt Trueblood said.

He heard the voice and looked up to see his friend standing ahead of him on the trail. Matt Trueblood was dressed in jeans, black T-shirt with a photograph of a fighter jet, and black cowboy boots. He held a beer in his hand.

"You're dead," Tobias said.

"Then why are you talking to me?"

"But you can't be here," Tobias said.

"Then I must be a hallucination."

"Yes."

Matt shrugged. "Even if I am, you still need to get up. My little girl is in trouble and you have to help her."

He looked at Matt accusingly. "You never said anything about her."

"I didn't know about her until she showed up on my doorstep. Do you honestly think I'm that kind of person? If I had known... but I didn't."

"She looks kind of like you," he said.

"Yeah. And now she's in trouble and you have to go help."

He got to his feet somehow, felt dizzy, but he forced himself to remain standing. Then a rush of nausea overwhelmed him and dropped to his knees again. For a moment he thought he would throw up but the nausea eased off. He felt pounding at the back of his head as he forced himself to get to his feet again.

Matt Trueblood was no longer there. He could have easily gone back to sleep, let the darkness take, but instead he took a step. Then another. Getting into the rhythm again and he knew it was mostly the drugs, but he actually felt stronger. He had to hurry because he knew he had limited time. The drugs would wear off and probably quicker than before.

He reached a creek and tried to keep to the dry part of the rocks going over, but his foot slipped on a rock and he went down. He caught himself on his hands, tearing them and drawing blood. He crawled through the water to the bank on the other side, shivering. He panted like a dog as he crawled in the wet ice and snow up the bank.

Trueblood was back with him again.

"You're wasting time. Get up. Stop playing in the water."

"Get away from me."

"I can't. My little girl is in trouble and you're still wasting time."

"I'm not wasting time. I can't do this."

"Yes, you can. You will. You'll do it for me. For her. For yourself. But you will do it."

He drew himself to his feet, knew with certainty that he had gone over the edge of madness and he might not be able to come back again. He wanted to punch his best friend, only his best friend was dead and a hallucination was talking to him. Or maybe it was another witch. The mountain seemed full of witches.

"It's the drugs, boy, "Matt Trueblood said. 'Those little pills that send you to happy land. They're killing you, but there's time for you to reach Micki. If you push yourself. You could make it if you push yourself."

"I'm trying," Tobias said.

"Try harder," Matt Trueblood said.

The old familiar taunt in Matt's voice. Try harder. Matt was always first in everything. He was bigger, stronger, and faster. He was smarter. He always had more success with girls. In high school, he was the quarterback, and in the Air Force Academy he had graduated highest in his class. In Vietnam, he had won the medal for taking his aircraft in harm's way to save a bunch of ground pounders and had been shot down. He took command on the ground and managed to get himself, and the grunts back to safety. He left behind no wounded or dead.

"Come on, "Matt said. You can do it. My little girl's up there."

"You didn't even know her name," he shouted.

"I told you I didn't even know she was alive. I would have told you, Swede. I would have gone to see her. It was just one weekend. Just one weekend in Paris and I fell in love with an actress and when the weekend was over, I proposed and she said I was a silly boy."

"She called you a silly boy?" Tobias said.

"That's what she said. She said go home, silly boy, so I went back home and she went back to her movies."

"You never told me."

"Some things weren't meant to be shared," Trueblood said. "So come on now, boy. Keep going. One leg after the other. Didn't they teach you toughness in the Marines?"

"I was tough," Tobias said.

"I know," Matt said. "That's why you did it, wasn't it? You wanted to prove how tough you were. You didn't have to prove it, Swede. I always knew it. Every time I turned around, you were there. Breathing on my neck. Making me run faster."

"You had to be first in everything," Tobias said.

"I couldn't let you beat me," Matt Trueblood admitted

"You even had to die first," Tobias said. "You cheated me even then."

"That wasn't my fault, partner," Matt said softly.

His anger at his old friend had taken his mind off the trail, off the snow, off the cold. He reached the last creek, went over it quickly and took the right trail. He wondered why he was so angry, why he was so full of the sense of being betrayed. His friend hadn't died on purpose. But he realized he had been feeling that betrayal ever since he opened his eyes and it was one of the reasons he hadn't wanted to talk about Matt with his daughter.

Matt stayed behind. He stopped, realizing he was walking by himself and he turned to look back at the creek. Matt was standing at the edge and he was fading away, a white vapor in the snow.

"We never had a chance to say goodbye," Tobias said.

"The drugs are wearing off," Matt said. "But she's up there. And so is Gus Creel. I can't go any farther."

"You should have said goodbye," Tobias said, but his friend was gone and he was aware of the pain again, in his lower back, muscles starting to tighten up. The pain helped clear a little of the fog from his mind and he put his hand in his pocket and gripped his pistol as he started up the trail again.

CHAPTER TWENTY TWO

Miraculously, he found his rhythm. For the first time since he had awakened from the coma, he moved out of the awkward crablike motion. The tightness in his calves loosened up and he was able to straighten up. It was still painful and he was still slow. He would never be fast again, but at least his brain was sending the right impulses to his muscles.

It was all about synapses, his doctors had told him. Lilly Creel had knocked a home run, right out of the ballpark, with all the force and beauty of the home run David Justice had hit in the old Fulton County Stadium to give the Braves the World Series win.

She had done it with a rusty shovel she had found lying in a heap of trash behind the Creel Café. The shovel was short and broken, but it was enough.

The doctors had him he was lucky, at that, because she could have hit him with the edge and sliced his head open.

Lucky.

Only the deep, dark blackness and waking up not remembering who he was or where he was or what had happened.

And missing his best friend.

Come on, Tobias, he thought. One foot in front of the other. Keep moving. Don't stop. One foot ahead of the other.

Cold seeping through his clothes, cold running down his spine and water seeping into his boots and soaking his shoes and chilling his toes.

Supposed to be waterproof boots. Supposed to be waterproof socks, for that matter.

One foot after the other.

All a matter of synapses. His synapses were like an electric current running through his body. Only the blow had short-circuited his synapse, had blocked them so that he his muscles didn't get the right message anymore. Tell a toe to move and his eyelid would blink. Tell a leg to go forward and it would go backwards. He was awkward, silly looking, like the scarecrow in the Wizard of Oz.

And even worse was that the thoughts didn't come naturally. He had to think about it before it happened. Nothing was natural. He thought about it now, pushed himself a little faster.

He reached yet another small creek crossing and he had to stop to gasp for breath. His lungs were burning. He stepped carefully into the water, picking his way across the slippery rocks. He didn't slip this time, but the icy water came up over his boots and they were definitely not acting as if they were waterproof.

He found Micki at the bottom of the trail. She was crumpled like a rag doll and he first thought she was dead, but then she reached one arm up and pulled herself up the trail a few inches. Her other arm hung uselessly by her side. She was trying to climb back up the hill with the last of her strength. He knelt by her, knew there was nothing he could really do. Her eyes blinked at him.

"He's got her chained up at the top of the hill," she said. "She's alive."

"I've got to get you help,' he said.

"Don't worry about me," she said. "He may take her again to someplace we can't find. Go get her now."

You're hurt," he said.

Amazingly, she laughed. "Yeah, he's really strong, Swede. I got him with my first shot, but he's also very quick. He picked me up and threw me like a Frisbee. I think he gets first prize for distance. I think he also broke my arm."

"Where is he?"

"I don't know. Maybe he's still up there. But he's got Sharon chained to an old army cot in a lean-to. Get to her, Swede."

"I've got to get help for you."

She grabbed his arm. "What you've got to do is get up that hill and get that child before he does anything to her. She's scared, Swede. We have to help her. The deputies are coming. I know it. Help her first."

He left her reluctantly. He climbed the trail the last few hundred feet and reached the top. Gus Creel no longer had the child chained to the cot in the lean-to. He had released her and now he held her in his massive arms. He was standing in the center of the plateau looking up at the sun. He seemed to be chanting something, but his words were unintelligible.

From somewhere behind Tobias heard a helicopter and he looked up to see one cross above the plateau. He knew it could not land, but it hovered above them for a moment and then darted off toward home. He hoped the pilot was talking to people on the ground. He hoped Abercorn had the entire National Guard battalion on the way up the hill. He looked again at the area where the helicopter had disappeared. He doubted Barry Silverman was the pilot. Silverman would not have guts enough to fly the helicopter in this weather.

"You see that chopper, Gus," Tobias said. "They're going to be coming for you. You can't get away this time. The Army and deputies are going to be all over this mountain, and they know where you are. You can't get away."

"Get off my mountain," he said.

"I'll leave, Gus. I'll leave, but let me take the child with you. She hasn't hurt you."

"The child stays with me. She's been chosen."

"You can't keep her, Gus."

"I am Kalanu," he said.

"Your name is Gus Creel," Tobias said. "I've known you since you played linebacker for the high school. You were pretty good. You remember the Red Devils, Gus. You remember Friday nights and cheerleaders and cold beer. You remember your brothers and sisters."

"I am Kalanu," he said, "and you can't harm me. I can see above the clouds."

"I don't think you will really turn into a raven," Tobias said. "And that's the only way you're going to get away. Now let me take Sharon away from here. She's cold, Gus. She's probably already sick."

Gus ignored him and moved slowly toward the edge of the embankment, and lifted his arms to the sky. The child in his arms moaned and struggled a little, but then was still. Tobias put his hand in his pocket, but he didn't pull the gun. He didn't want to force Creel into doing anything when he still had a chance to talk to him.

Gus Creel was a mess. His clothes were nearly rotted off him and clung to his massive body in long strips. He was covered all over with insect bites and scratches. His dark hair was long and shaggy and dirty. At a distance he was hairy enough to pass for a bear or
the legendary Sasquatch.

"Put her down, Gus," Tobias said softly. "You really don't want to hurt her."

Tobias moved closer. From somewhere there was a rifle shot, and another answering shot in the distance. It was obvious that rescuers were on the move, following the few narrow trails toward the top, and equally obvious they were moving to surround the area.

"Please put her down, Gus," Tobias said again. "Think about what you are doing. Think about the café, Gus. Think about getting a hot shower and some food. Think about being warm again. You don't have to stay up here."

"I am the spirit of the mountain," he insisted. "I am the Raven."

"No," Tobias said. "You're Gus Creel. You're not a witch. You're just a man who's hurting inside and you need to come home. There are people who care for you, Gus. So why don't you put Sharon down and come home?"

Tobias hardly thought about what he was saying. He only wanted to keep Gus talking, to keep him from doing anything violent. His pistol was his last resort, and he was terrified of using it. There was no way of getting a killing shot with Sharon in his arms, and what if his synapses decided to go haywire when he started to fire. He had just a good a chance of hitting her.

He wished Matt Trueblood was back and Matt could sneak up and hit him in the head from behind, but he supposed there was just so much one could ask of hallucinations.

"Come on, Gus. Don't do anything stupid."

Tobias noticed the blood then. It was on Gus's lower right side, just above his thigh. Micki's shot was low, but it was a solid hit. A little lower or higher and Gus might not have been walking around. It was actually a little hard to see how he was moving about anyway.

"Your mother is worried about you, Gus," Tobias said. "Miss April is concerned. She wants you to come home."

Sharon Bishop cried out and Tobias realized that Gus's powerful hands had been squeezing her too tight, and Tobias knew his strength was capable of crushing her ribcage; of squeezing the life from her. He had no choice and he started to draw his pistol out, but Creel had the instinctive savagery of a wild animal, and sensed his danger. He dropped Sharon Bishop and he rushed at Tobias, incredibly fast, like an unstoppable freight train.

His pistol caught on the inner lining of his pocket and then it was too late for anything else because Creel smashed into him.

CHAPTER TWENTY THREE

Creel was incredibly fast and strong and when he hit Tobias, Tobias went backwards and hit the ground hard. At the very last moment he had managed to rip his pistol out of his pocket, but the impact had sent the pistol spinning away from him. He had no idea where it ended up, and he had no chance to look for it.

He was stunned for a moment. His head cleared a second before Creel started to stomp him. He frantically rolled over and over, trying to avoid Creel's violent kicks. He managed to catch Creel around the leg and jerked but Creel never lost his balance and instead brought his other boot around in a solid, sweeping kick that caught him in the stomach and lifted him off the ground. He handed a half dozen feet away on top of a broken tree branch. He somehow managed to scramble to his feet with the tree branch in his hand. He pointed it toward Creel as the big man rushed again, and the man's own momentum drove him into the jagged edge. The tree branch shattered into splinters, but he had hurt Creel, at least a little.

Creel slowed a little cautiously but he was still coming after Tobias. Tobias backed up looking for another weapon he could use. Tobias was close enough to smell his rancid breath and the smell of wood smoke and sweat. It was nauseating. He moved in a circle around the clearing, hoping to get back to the area where he had lost the pistol. His heart was pounding rapidly and he knew he was going to have to do something soon because he was not capable of fighting Creel for very long.

"Listen to me," Tobias said. "Listen to me, Gus. You're sick and you need help. There are doctors who can help."

"I'm Kalanu," Gus said.

"You're not listening to me,' Tobias said as Gus Creel rushed at him again.

There was a glittering madness in Gus Creel's eyes, and a savage rage, but this time Tobias was able to avoid his rush. Creel's hands grasped the back of his coat as he twisted away and he felt something tear, but he slipped away to the other side of the plateau.

It was a game that was not going to end well.

He did not have the strength for it.

Another rush, another near miss.

The third time he stumbled and Creel wrapped his arms around him and picked him up from behind, but Creel had him around the waist and his arms were still free. He reached behind his head, grabbed Creel by his greasy hair and jerked. Creel tightened his grip. Tobias gasped as felt the enormous pressure, felt his ribs beginning to give way. He released Creel's hair and in one last desperate attempt, poked his fingers at where he thought Creel's eyes would be.

And got lucky.

One finger into the middle of Creel's eye and the big man bellowed in rage and for a moment the pressure of his arms eased and Tobias slipped down to his knees. He crawled away. He lacked the strength to get to his feet and Creel caught him in moments. Creel kicked him and he rolled, somehow getting to his feet again. He blocked a savage fist from Creel but couldn't block the second one and it caught him above his eye.

Not the head, he thought. Oh, please, not the head.

He staggered backwards and Creel followed. He went into a boxer's stance, jabbed with his left hand and struck a solid blow with his right. Creel brushed it away like he would brush away a fly and kept coming. He kept backing away, jabbing with his fist to keep Creel away. He stumbled over another tree limb and Creel was on him.

This time Creel jerked him around and closed his arms around him so that he had no chance of using his hands.

The unyielding pressure began again. Tobias desperately brought his knee up between Creel's legs, but the big man only grunted. Tobias did it again twice more, but it was if the man did not feel it.

But then Creel lifted him off the ground as he changed his deadly grip and Tobias was able to reach his nose with his teeth. Tobias fought back the nausea as he tried to bite Creel's nose off.

The man squealed and released Tobias the second time. Tobias hit his back and looked up. Creel was bleeding from his nose and yelping but then he came after Tobias again. Tobias tried to crawl away, but there wasn't a chance. This time Gus Creel kicked him in the side and lifted him up off the ground. He kicked him again, and this time Creel kicked him solidly in the head and the entire world went sort of fuzzy.

Not the head, damn it, Tobias thought. Not again.

But the kick came again, solid and deadly, jerking his head back. He tasted blood and he knew it was over. He was dizzy and sick and the synapses weren't working right again. He couldn't make his legs move. He knew he was on his back and he was looking up at the bloodied face of Gus Creel. He was lying on something uncomfortable and he wished he had the energy to move away.

Gus Creel's face was in kind of a cloud. He couldn't make out his features exactly anymore.

But he saw the indistinct shape that came up behind Gus Creel, heard the savage cry and saw the flash of the knife as she drove it into Creel's back, and then another cry of rage and pain from Creel.

It was Micki and she had somehow managed to pull herself up that slick hill with one arm and she had used that deadly looking knife on him. But it still wasn't enough. Creel jerked away and the knife was left in his side and then he stepped forward and lifted her up with one hand, twisting her broken arm again. Micki sobbed in pain.

"No," Tobias said.

He lifted up, somehow, got to his knees and looked down stupidly at what he had been lying on. Micki's pistol. She had lost it when Creel hurled her down the hill the first time. He looked back at Micki and Gus. He was killing her now, squeezing her in that terrible, deadly embrace.

"Stop," he said. 'Stop."

He kept saying it over and over as he picked up the pistol and fired it until it was empty.

CHAPTER TWENTY FOUR

Tobias had very little memory of the trip back down the mountain, only that it was miserable. The Army paramedics had not known about the pain pills he had already taken, and they gave him an additional shot of morphine. It turned the world a lot of different colors. They could not rig a proper stretcher for the narrow trail, and they half-dragged and half-carried him down to the base camp. With enough men arriving, they had cleared out the area where Micki's chopper had crashed, and a very brave civilian pilot had brought in his helicopter twice to fly them all off the mountain.

Every time Tobias was coherent, he tried to ask about Micki and the little girl, but people just kept telling him to relax and everything would be all right. Deep down Tobias knew they were wrong. He had been hit in the head again. The doctors had warned him of additional injury. Deep down, he thought things would not ever be all right.

Hospitals rooms are a lot alike, but when he opened his eyes, he knew he was in his same room in the hospital in Gainesville, the room where he had spent so much time, so much of it unconscious. It had the same beige colored walls with a little water leak on one corner, and it had the same yellow curtains.

He was in and out of sleep for a while. When he was awake, he watched Tracy Clavier on the news. It was a good story and she presented it well. Helicopter crashes and a deadly shootout and the rescue of a little girl. It was good until she got to the part where Gus Creel had not been found. There were lots of blood trails. A statement from Sheriff Abercorn said he believed Gus Creel could not survive his wounds and the weather, but he was considered armed and dangerous.

The nurse who came into the room and took his blood pressure and temperature was also familiar. He had not known her name, but she was petite, mid-forties, with heavy breasts that strained at the tight uniform she wore when she leaned over to take

170

the thermometer from his mouth. He also noticed she had a nameplate, Carol.

"Am I going to live?" He asked.

She didn't smile. "The doctor will have to tell you that."

"You don't have any opinion?" Tobias said.

"Don't give me a hard time," she said. "You were such a good patient before."

"I was in a coma before," he said.

"Exactly," she said.

His doctor was not familiar and he thought he had met them all. Doctor James Lee was a portly man with thinning white hair and a booming voice. His white jacket had coffee stains and a pen in his pocket had leaked and showed a blue stain. He did not look like anybody's idea of a skilled doctor, and yet Tobias felt an immediate confidence in him.

"I didn't get a chance to see you when you were in before," he said, looking at Tobias's chart at the end of the bed. "You were quite the talk around the hospital. People were giving odds that you weren't going to wake up."

"I'm glad I was some entertainment," Tobias said.

"Yes, you're a very entertaining fellow. You're the talk of the town. You're a sure enough walking around miracle, son."

"Am I?"

"Well, it wasn't medicine that pulled you through the first time. You were dead. All we did was hook you up to some machines that kept you breathing and going to the bathroom, and then we waited for you to die."

"That's comforting,' he said.

"You know how money this hospital spent keeping you alive?"

"No idea."

"A hell of a lot. I might have operated on ten people for the money it took to keep you alive. So yes, you're a bloody miracle."

"I get the feeling you're not happy with me,' Tobias said.

"I think you should stop letting people hit you in the head."

"It sounds like good advice."

Doctor Lee sat down on the edge of his bed.

"I read all about you the last time you were in here. You were in Vietnam, right. Two purple hearts?"

"Yes."

"I was with the First Calvary myself. I pulled enough bullets and shrapnel out of guys like you to build a factory. You've done enough. The next time somebody hits you in the head, you're going to be sipping soup through a straw and you're not going to remember your name. You were lucky this time, but your head isn't right. Something is all mixed up in there and it may not ever work right again."

"So what are you telling me?"

"You may not ever get well this time. Not completely. Right now your blood pressure's fine and you haven't been getting the headaches and there's a possibility you could maybe live another thirty years."

"Maybe?"

"Nothing is definite about the practice of medicine," Doctor Lee said. "But there's other stuff you need to know. Like you're probably never going to drive a car again and you will have occasional blackouts, and you will have the headaches. You may even lose some of your basic motor skills. Your days of behaving like a sheriff in the Wild West are over."

"I wasn't behaving like a wild west sheriff. I had to do what I had to do. You act like I enjoy getting hit in the head."

"No. But when they brought you in here, I didn't think you were going to make it. Your blood pressure was sky high and you were white as a sheet. You were having hallucinations. By the way, didn't anybody warn you of the side effects of medication that you were taking? We had to pump your stomach to get it all out of you."

"I knew what they were. I had to get up that mountain. It was the only way."

"Everybody appreciates what you and Micki Trueblood did up there," Doctor Lee said. "But you are not physically capable of doing those things anymore." Doctor Lee made a few more notations on the chart and stood up. "I'm going to keep you here for a few days, but there's no point in you being here if everything looks good. Right now it looks good."

"Thanks," Tobias said dryly.

Doctor Lee stopped at the door to Tobias's room.

"You ever remember hearing about the John Wayne syndrome when you were in Vietnam?"

"Yeah," Tobias said.

"A guy thinks he's John Wayne. He thinks he's some kind of hero. He charges up with his guns blazing and he generally gets himself killed."

"I get your point, doctor," Tobias said.

"I hope you do. Because you know the really bad part about a guy who has the John Wayne syndrome?"

"What's that?"

"He so often gets his friends killed."

CHAPTER TWENTY FIVE

Carol came back in shortly and gave him something to help him sleep. He slept and dreamed of his grandfather. They were back on the mountain, he and Matt Trueblood and his grandfather. It was late and dark and they sat by the fire, and his grandfather told his stories and he and Matt shivered in delicious fright as every shadow outside the campfire became a warrior with a blood-soaked knife.

When he awoke, Abby was there.

He smelled her scent before he opened his eyes. She sat primly in a chair farthest from the bed. Her legs were crossed. She wore a blue form-fitting dress, hose and heels. Her hair was down and she had on lipstick.

"How are you feeling?" she asked.

"I'm awake," he said.

"Yes," she said. "I was a little afraid sitting here watching you. It reminded me of all the times I did before. They told me you were okay and just sleeping, but it's a relief to see you open your eyes."

"I know this is all been hard on you, Abby," he said.

"You'll never know how hard," she said. "I hate this place. I hate this room. For a long time I hated you."

"I understand," he said.

"No, you don't. You were starting to get better. Now I think it's probably going to start over again with the headaches and the pain and the therapy."

He heard the accusation in her voice.

"Abby," he said.

"I can't do this anymore," she said. "I hate the sight of this hospital. I hate this room. I came every day, at first, you know. Every day I did all the things a good wife is supposed to do when her husband is in a coma and nobody knows if he'll ever wake up again. I read to you. I talked to you. I bathed you. And I watched you shrink away to nothing but skin and bones. You looked like one of those pictures you see of the Jews in the concentration camps. You looked like death."

"It's going to get better, Abby," he said.

She shook her head. "It can't get better. I love you, Swede. I love you and I hate you and I hate myself. I know you probably can't understand that."

"I think I do," he said.

"I thought I was a person with a good moral compass. I thought I had values. I thought I was strong enough to handle whatever life had for me. I was wrong. I wasn't any of those things and I blamed you for it. I blamed you for my own failures."

There were things he wanted to say to her … promises of how things would be like they had been. But they never would because he would never be the man he was.

"Maybe we could take a little vacation or something. We'll go to the beach. You know how they always say people from the mountains go to the beach for vacation and people who live on the beach go to the mountains."

"It's not working, Swede."

"There's still a chance."

"No. I can't spend the rest of my life feeling guilty and I would every time I looked at you. I cheated on you, Swede. I went with another man because I was lonely and hurt and angry."

"We make mistakes, Abby. I've made enough. We can work through this."

"No. You were sick for so long. I thought you were going to die. I felt as if my life was over before it began."

"We can try, Abby."

"It's gone too far," Abby said.

"Are you in love with this man?"

"Hardly," she said. "No, it wasn't about love and it's over with anyway. It's finished. But it's finished between us also. I know that. I want a divorce, Swede."

He had heard the words before and he had hoped not to hear them again. In a way he had thought it was his last chance with Abby.

"I'm sorry, Swede," Abby said.

She came to the bed and leaned over and kissed him gently on the lips. Her perfume stayed in the room afterwards, lingering around his head. He took a deep breath of her perfume and closed his eyes, and drifted into sleep.

CHAPTER TWENTY SIX

When he opened his eyes again, Harvey Abercorn was there. Harvey was in a new blue suit, but he was getting crumbs on it from a sugary doughnut he was eating. Tobias smelled coffee.

"Is that from the Mountain Laurel?" Tobias asked.

"Fresh made this morning," Harvey agreed, as he finished off the last bite. "I would have saved you one but I had no idea when you were going to wake up. I could have died of starvation sitting here."

"You're a real sweetheart, Harvey," Tobias said.

"That's what everybody says, Swede."

"So how are Micki and Sharon Bishop? Nobody seems to want to tell me."

"I'm surprised Micki hasn't been around to see you. She looks kind of funny in her big cast. Everybody at the station signed it. She's really in better shape than you are."

"And Sharon Bishop?"

"She's alive, Swede. She's a tough little girl. Do you remember anything she did up there?"

"No."

"You and Micki both were out of it for a while. I mean, we had deputies and the army on the move but we were still thirty minutes away when we heard the gunshots. That little girl somehow pulled you all together in a short of pile and snuggled down between you and covered you all with her blankets. It was good thinking on her part and it kept you warm enough until we got there."

'So how is she now?" Tobias said.

"It's hard to say. Physically, she's okay but her momma says she jumps at every sound and she's not sleeping well, and she has to have the lights on. I don't know, Swede. Hopefully, one day she'll get over being afraid of the dark."

"There are always scars," Tobias said.

"Yes."

177

"And the ones that are the worse are the ones you can't see."

Harvey nodded his head. "We still don't know about Gus Creel, but he's got to be dead. It's freezing up on Kalanu and six inches of snow has fallen higher up. He was stabbed and shot. I mean, Micki hit him once and you had to have hit him at least a couple of times with five shots, even as bad as you shoot."

"Funny man," Tobias said.

"We'll find him when the weather warms up," Harvey said.

"I hope so," Tobias said. "I know I don't want to chase him around that mountain anymore."

"On the good side of the news, I had a long, long talk with Deputy Art Palmer. He has decided to resign from the department and go to work in his brother's hadware store."

"So Gail's been reinstated," Tobias said.

"With back pay," Abercorn said. "And we're going to get that door fixed in the back. It's incredible to me that Clyde Jessop could have reached the end of that ladder to climb up that building. He must have had some kind of adrenaline rush going on."

"We've both seen some strange things."

Harvey looked decidedly uncomfortable.

"What?" Tobias said.

"I guess there's no way of saying this but plain. I'm going to have to ask you to resign, Tobias. The truth is you've reached retirement age and you've got a good pension, and the chances are you're not coming back to work."

"You know something I don't," Tobias said.

"Come on, Swede. You know you're not at your best. It wasn't fair of me to use you in the way I did, but I didn't think I had a choice. But I would have been responsible for you, being dead on that mountain. And Micki. It was a very close call."

"I was there, remember?"

"Yes. But my point is you shouldn't have been."

"I'm not your responsibility."

"Everything is my responsibility," Abercorn said. "I'm the sheriff. Sometimes you forget that makes me the boss. But I'm also your friend. Now your marriage is ruined … again. And you nearly got yourself killed. You need to take some time and go fishing or something."

"You're bringing in a new investigator," Tobias asked.

"I'm going to do some interviews, but I'll probably give the job to Owen," Abercorn said.

"Okay," Tobias said.

"And there's something else."

"Yes?"

"The doctor says you might not recover completely from this last time being hit in the head. He says this second injury may permanently disable you."

"He didn't tell me that."

"He thought it might be better coming from me. So now I have that also to trouble my sleep. Look, Swede, you've been the best investigator I've ever known, and half the county right now is singing your praises about what you and Micki did on that mountain."

"Only half?" Tobias said.

"Well, the other half of the county is Creels and they all hate you."

"True."

"It's also unpleasant for me right now. A lot of people are calling for my head. You were on medical leave. You weren't supposed to be working. That female reporter from Gainesville is crucifying the two of us every chance she gets. And I have a damned helicopter to pay for."

"It crashed in the line of duty," Tobias said.

"Try telling that to Silverman and Creel. Both of them are so cheap they'd have us doing patrol work on mules. It's going to be a nasty political fight to get them to pay and this time I might not even survive. Helicopters are expensive."

"Then maybe I'll run for Sheriff,' Tobias said.

"You're welcome to run and you might even win, but you'd hate the job."

He knew it was true. He had always hated the politics of police work. He could not crunch numbers for budgets all day long, or make pretty speeches to business groups or the ladies book club.

"Okay, Harvey. I'll stay out of sight and out of mind for a while. But you don't care if I do a little last minute investigating, just between you and me?"

"What's on your mind?" Harvey asked suspiciously.

"There's pieces of the puzzle that doesn't fit together. We know that Gus Creel met Sharon Bishop through her mother and when he started going crazy, he fixated on her. I don't know what he had in mind for her, and I'm not sure he knew himself, but I'm sure he wasn't coherent enough to make a phone call to Sharon's mother."

"So you already said that you thought someone else made the call," Abercorn shrugged. "Another member of the family."

"Yeah, I thought that. I still do. But why? The last thing they wanted was to be associated with Gus and the kidnapping. I am sure there's still going to be some repercussions to anyone named Creel. Someone is sure to bring up the connection in the future. So why call attention by making a phone call."

"I don't understand," Harvey said.

"Unless there was something else going on at the same time. Maybe the kidnapping really had nothing to do with the phone call and the objection to the Windfall Project being started up again."

"So what?"

"What do you think is the real objection to the Windfall Project?"

"It's environmental. People want to keep things the way they were."

"Maybe. But it started me thinking."

Harvey shrugged. "Where are you going with this? The board of commissioners is very big on the environment. Creel is a big environment man and so is Silverman."

"But neither of them are really the save the whales type," Tobias pointed out.

"Not really, I still don't see your point."

"How much money you think the Creel's make from moonshine?"

"Come on, Tobias. You know that's a sore spot. You've been trying to close their still down for years, but they still get a lot

180

of protection and there's really not much money in it. It's probably not worth a few thousand to them every year. It's not like the old days. I actually think they just do it to make us mad."

"Or to make us look in another direction," Tobias said. "In the old days the Creel made a fortune in moonshine. They had regular runs to Atlanta and they sold to the nightclubs."

"There's just not that kind of money in moonshine anymore."

"So where is the real money," Tobias asked.

"In drugs," Harvey said, and he went a little pale.

"There are a lot of acres up on Kalanu Mountain. Especially near the old Falls. There are few hiking trails in that area. It's not easy to reach and not easy to see from the air. That's part of the Windfall Project, to clean that area up. To build new hiking trails. To make it more accessible to the population."

"You're saying they're growing weed up there," Harvey said.

"I think it's a definite possibility you should look into. The Windfall Project would bring a lot of new eyes to that area."

Harvey shook his head. "But we would have known. There would have been some kind of indication. One of our snitches would have said something if the Creels were into growing that kind of stuff."

"Maybe. Maybe not. But I don't think Creel's real passion is about saving the environment and this is the only thing that makes sense to me."

With a grin, Harvey said, "you know this could be priceless, Swede. I'm starting to think you're right. If you are, there's going to be a lot of very embarrassed people and it will be the final straw for Creel. He could not be elected dog catcher. Plus, I expect Silverman will be quick to throw him under the bus. If you're right, I'll get two helicopters."

"I'm right," Tobias said. "It's the only thing that makes sense."

Harvey Abercorn seldom looked excited about anything, but he was getting a little red in the face.

"We'll get some guys together. If those fields are there, we'll find. I'll take Jack Mathis and that Carp fellow, and a few more deputies. Of course we could find it faster if we had Micki up in a helicopter. Maybe she could borrow one."

Tobias shrugged. "Might be a good idea."

Harvey looked a lot more enthusiastic and less bone-weary than when he had come through the door. His face was animated. He touched Tobias's shoulder.

"You're still the best detective I know, Swede."

Harvey left him alone. He heard the soft swish of the door closing. He was suddenly very tired, but he didn't feel as if he could sleep. His mind was working really fast. He spent a long time looking up at the stain on the ceiling and smiling.

CHAPTER TWENTY SEVEN

Micki was the last one who came. She didn't show up until the day he was released from the hospital and she brought underwear, jeans, shoes, a red flannel shirt and a light jacket. The clothes were all new and freshly laundered.

"Did you hear the news?" Micki asked.

"Yes. You were busy yesterday."

"Estimate is more than a couple of million dollars' worth of pot growing up by the fall. Now everybody's excited. Even better, criminal charges are being filed against several Creel family members. You did well, Swede."

"Me?"

"Sheriff Abercorn gave you the credit in a press conference this morning. It probably didn't make the Creels appreciate you anymore, but a lot of other people do. Including the Governor. There's talk of giving you some kind of award."

"Probably a gold watch," Tobias said a little bitterly.

Micki studied him curiously. "Feeling a little sorry for yourself?"

"I'm not quite ready to be put out to pasture."

For days the weather had been clearing up. There had been two solid days of warmth and sunlight, but that morning the temperature had dropped again and the weatherman talked about snow flurries.

The standing joke about North Georgia weather was that if you didn't like it, wait until the afternoon and it would change.

Micki wore a dress. He didn't think he'd actually seen her in a dress before. It was a dark grey and form fitting and came to her knees. Her black hair was loose to her shoulders. She wore another pair of calfskin knee-high calfskin boots but they were fancier, black with fringe trimming. She had on a touch of lipstick and her fingernails were painted.

She wore a lightweight cast on her left arm but it didn't seem to hamper her. She didn't have it pinned and moved it freely. She seemed to have little discomfort.

"Second cast," Micki said, noticing his glance. "The first one was like an iron halter. It really itched. But I heal fast. The doctor put me in this one just this morning and it's a little like getting out of jail. I can drive and everything."

The nurse came for him a wheelchair. He did not protest. He had learned this particular nurse was tough and inflexible. She rolled him down the hallway to the elevator and down to the exit. Another Kalanu County Sheriff's vehicle was at the curb.

"So you're still a member of the club," Tobias said.

"Yes," Micki said. "And they decided to buy the helicopter. Especially when Sharon Bishop's father, in his uniform and medals, made a speech about how much he appreciated the brave heroes who risked life and limb to save his daughter. He wished there was some way he could show his appreciation."

"Brave heroes, huh," Tobias said.

"Yes, that would be us."

He stood up and the nurse started to wheel his chair back inside.

"I hope I was as good a patient as last time," he said.

The nurse almost smiled before she disappeared back through the electronic doors.

"Friendly lady," Micki said.

"She's a real sweetheart," Tobias said.

Piled in the back of the sheriff's unit were a lot of boxes packed with stuff and several hangers of clothing hanging from hooks. One box was open and he saw it was full of plaques and memorabilia that had once hung in his office in the house he shared with Abby.

"You've been busy," he said.

"Abby called me and asked if I would help move you out. I was amazed she would ask for my help, but I went. It took me three trips but I moved all of your stuff to your grandfather's old cabin on Mount Rawls. This is the last of it."

"Thanks."

"So it's really over between you two."

"She says she wants a divorce," Tobias said.

Micki shrugged. "If it's any consolation to you, Abby was pretty miserable. She'd been crying. I don't think this is very easy on her, either."

Tobias nodded. Micki started the car and pulled away from the hospital curb. She drove carefully through the parking lot and turned right out of the hospital entrance. She drove a hundred yards and turned right again, this time onto the highway leading out of Gainesville toward Mount Rawls.

"Did you know about Abby?" Tobias asked.

"Know what?"

"That she was having an affair?"

Micki sighed. "Pretty much everyone knew. I almost told you a couple of times but I didn't have the courage, and maybe I didn't figure it was any of my business. I'm not really family, am I? Besides, I come from a background where affairs of the heart are pretty normal. Believe me, parties at my mother's house could be quite an education sometimes."

He was quiet for a while. He watched the passing scenery. He thought of his busted marriages and how mostly it had been about his job, and how he had not been able to give emotionally to his wives what the needed or wanted. Now he had no job, and no wife. There had been no children.

"Still feeling sorry for yourself?" Micki said, sensing his mood.

"Just thinking about things," Tobias said.

"You have a gift, Swede," she said. "You see things other people don't. The business about the cigarette probably saved Gail Mathis's career. You understood there was something else going on with the Windfall Project before anyone else."

"Abercorn would have seen it if he hadn't had so many other worries on his mind."

"He might have. Maybe. But the point is you do see it, and you've been doing it for most of your life. You've put a lot of bad people in jail. You've saved a lot of lives. You saved Sharon Bishop's life."

"*We* saved her life," Tobias said.

"But that should give a good feeling about yourself," she said. "Believe me. I know a lot of people who have everything they ever desired, fame and fortune, and at the end of the day they have to get high to feel good about themselves."

"You're trying to cheer me up," he said.

"I'm just telling you the truth. Of course, you'll still probably end up sitting in front of the courthouse ogling the pretty girls in stretch pants and drooling, but that comes to all of us. It's called old age. But you should be proud of what you've done."

"I never drool," he protested.

"So lighten up," Micki said. "You've got a few good years left before that happens and I expect Sheriff Abercorn will be calling on you again. And before that, when you are feeling better, I want you to take me camping up on Kalanu Mountain. I want to sit around a campfire and hear the old stories your grandfather used to tell. I've been talking to Hattie."

"Mad Hattie?"

"Yes, we've been making plans for a weekend. She knows just the place. "

It sounded good to him. To be back on the mountain again in warmer weather, to sit by the fire, to reminiscence about old times. Except this time Matt Trueblood wouldn't be there.

"In the meantime, that cabin of your grandfather's?" Micki said.

"Yes."

"When people told me your grandfather had an old cabin, I thought of something like a rustic looking place in the woods. It's in the woods all right, but it's not very rustic."

"My grandfather liked his comforts."

"It's like the Disneyland of cabins," Micki said. "What did your grandfather need with six bedrooms?"

"He made a lot of money with his lectures. People visited. Did you see the back bedroom with the closet?"

"I looked around a little. I don't remember a closet."

"There's a closet in there. There are autographs on the wall of famous people who came and stayed in the cabin. You might have known some of the people."

"Me? Why?'

"John Wayne's name is on there, along with quite a few other actors who made movies in the area. There are a couple of Presidents who signed. There are several local dignitaries. Lewis Gizzard and Hershel Walker. My grandfather knew and was friends with a great many famous people."

"I don't know about John Wayne, but I might be interested if Brad Pitt's name is up there."

"Afraid not," Tobias said.

'Then the wall is not complete yet," Micki said.

She stopped at an intersection at a red light and then made another turn onto Atlanta Highway. It was now a straight line to Mount Rawls. There was only one other turn-off to make, up the narrow road and across a couple of creeks to his grandfather's cabin.

"I saw your father up there on the mountain," Tobias said. "I saw Matt."

Micki glanced at him. "You were hallucinating. You might have told me you took an entire bottle of pills."

"It was only a few pills, and it was the only way. But the hallucination seemed very real."

"I've never had a hallucination myself, but don't they all seem very real?"

"I suppose. But seeing your father made me realize how angry I was at him."

"I don't understand," Micki said.

"Because he died," Tobias said.

Micki was silent for a few moments. He noticed she drove a little more cautiously with the broken arm, but the road was nearly deserted anyway. The sky was thick with clouds, the kind of clouds that might mean heavy snow.

"I had a dog once when I was a little girl," Micki said. "I kept him for a long time but he got sick, and one day I came home and the dog wasn't there anymore. My mother had him put to sleep because he was old and nasty and messy. I couldn't blame my mother. I had to blame the dog."

"Yes," Tobias said.

"You didn't want to talk about him with me because you were mad at him."

"Yes," Tobias admitted.

"And now?"

"I'm still kind of mad at him," Tobias said. "I told him up on the mountain. I never had a chance to say goodbye. And because I needed to talk to him after I came out of that coma. You see, I could say things to him I couldn't say to anyone else. He would understand. Everybody else might think I was crazy, but we'd been talking crazy things to each other since my grandfather brought him home that day."

"I know so little about him," Micki said. "I want to know so much. I know he was married to his high school sweetheart. I know everybody liked him, but when you ask what he was like, they say, 'Oh, he was nice. He was a nice man.' But I want to know who he was."

"I understand," Tobias said.

"Do you? Do you really? You know when I came here, I didn't want to do anything but see him. I just wanted to see what he looked like and what his life was life. But I found this place, I found this mountain and it was like coming home. It was like the mountains were crying out to me, to the part of me that was wild and savage and real. So I introduced myself. You know how I did that?"

"How?"

"I followed him one day to the hospital, to your room. He was reading to you. He went every day. I walked in and he took one look at me and he knew. The resemblance was just too obvious. And I am not sure he ever got over his love of my mother. But we talked, a little. And I started going every day when he visited you. Mostly he didn't talk. I simply sat and listened to him read to you. He took me over to Blairsville to meet one of his daughters, my half-sister. It was an unpleasant meeting. A couple of days later his son showed up ranting and raving about me. It seemed neither of them cared for an interloper showing up who might have some claim on their father's estate."

"You didn't mention that you were filthy rich," Tobias said.

"No, I didn't. Not to them, or my father. But he did find out I was also a pilot. He took me up in his helicopter and his piper cub

188

and he let me drive. And the next day he took me to his lawyer's office and I was made a full partner in his business. My siblings were not happy with that, but I think he knew then somehow his time was short and he wanted to leave his business to someone who would love flying as much as he did. "

'His children are not my favorite people," Tobias said. "I don't know how they turned out so different. Their mother was a gentle, caring person. So was Matt. "

"Who was my father?" Micki said. "I want to understand who he was."

"He was a hard luck kid," Tobias said. "His parents were hard luck people. They were the kind of people they write the maudlin country songs about. His dad was severely injured in a work accident when he was a young man. He took pills and booze to compensate for the pain so he was always out of it. His mom worked as house maid and cleaner for several homes around the mountain and she passed away fairly young. His dad was not capable of taking care of Matt, so we sort of adopted him. It was never official but he became my brother."

"My grandfather brought him home one night. He was bigger than I was, but he seemed sort of fragile somehow. He was dirty and in torn clothes and had bruises all over."

"His father?"

"Yes. The drinking led to beatings. But Matt loved him anyway. I guess all kids do. Deputies were called out to his home one night. Matt's father had finally taken too many pills and too much booze and ended up drowning in his own bathtub. My grandfather was at the station when they brought him in. Back then things were done a little differently. There were few social organizations controlling where children were put. My grandfather took him home. My mother fed him, put him in the tub, gave him a pair of my pajamas and put him to bed. He never left."

Micki reached over and touched the back of Tobias's hand. "Thank you. I know talking about him is hard. But I need to hear it. Do you understand?"

"Yes."

"And I'd like to get to know you," she said. I filled up the pantries and the refrigerator with enough food to last a month. I primed the generator and it's ready to go if needed. I moved my stuff into the little bedroom on the corner. I figured you could have the big bedroom."

"I take it you're planning on staying," Tobias said.

"For a while," Micki said. "Doctor Lee was concerned about you being by yourself. "

"You don't have to do this, Micki," he said.

"I want to do this. And there's beer and steak and popcorn and I found a lot of your movies. You don't have a lot of modern stuff, do you? I mean, a lot of your movies are black and white. You have a lot of musicals. And a lot of my mother's movies, some in the original Italian. Did either of you speak Italian?"

"No," Tobias admitted. "You know, I can get along all right, no matter what the doctor says. I can fix my own food and open my own drinks. I really can get along."

"I told you. I want to watch old movies with you. I want to talk about my father. "

"Okay," he said reluctantly.

"And besides, I'm afraid if I leave you alone long enough, you'll get married again."

He laughed out loud. It had been a long time since he laughed. They were close enough for him to look out the window and see Mount Rawls and only the shadow of Kalanu behind it. The weatherman was right. Snow flurries were starting again, and he knew it would be cold up on the mountain. He wondered if the spirit of the mountain was satisfied. He wondered if Gus Creel was still alive, somewhere huddled next to a fire. He hoped not. Gus Creel was someone he never wanted to meet again.

The snow became thicker, swirls of snow around the car blocking out the view of Kalanu Mountain, coating the world in a cover of white, and he thought that watching old movies and sipping wine by the warmth of his grandfather's enormous old fireplace with Matt Trueblood's daughter might indeed be a good way to say good-bye to his friend.

Made in the USA
Las Vegas, NV
16 August 2023